POOL FISHING
STORIES

BARBARA DEMARCO-BARRETT

iconic locales. A sure thing bestseller and a must-have summer read, *Palm Springs Noir* unquestionably brings the heat. Bravo!"

— Michael Thomas Barry, *New York Journal of Books*

"As editor DeMarco-Barrett points out, it's hard to think 'noir' in a landscape that offers 300 days of sunshine a year. But unrelenting heat and light can do funny things to your brain. An engaging mix of the good, the bad, and the off-kilter."

— *Kirkus*

"Forget pristine pastels and midcentury modern mojo. When it comes to the Coachella Valley, something ominous—even bloodstained—exists in the shadows of the glaring sun. DeMarco-Barrett, an Orange County resident and frequent valley visitor, has curated 14 short stories that delightfully raise eyebrows and keep your eyes feasting on the page."

— Greg Archer, *Palm Springs Desert Sun*

Praise for *Pen on Fire: A Busy Woman's Guide to Igniting the Writer Within*

"A wonderful mix of the practical and the inspirational, which can only come from a writer who knows what she's doing and what it takes to get things done."

— T. Jefferson Parker, author of *Desperation Reef*

"We all know what it's like to have that fierce drive to do something remarkable . . . and no idea where or how to start. *Pen on Fire* is a beginning writer's dream cocktail of fortitude: equal parts compassion, inspiration, and fabulous limbering exercises. Want to be a writer? Drink deeply of Barbara DeMarco-Barrett's hard-earned wisdom."

— Jodi Picoult, author of *By Any Other Name*

"*Pen on Fire* serves as a reminder that we can't get too precious or rigid about when/how/where we write. Whatever part of your practice you struggle with, you'll find yourself—and your solution—in this book. Got 15 minutes? Set a timer and let your pen burn up the page."

— Maggie Ginsberg, author of *Still True*

"So many people have told me they are burning to write but can't seem to find a spare moment. I wish I could track them all down now and hand each of them a copy of *Pen on Fire*."

— Gayle Brandeis, author of *Drawing Breath: Essays on Writing, the Body, and Loss*

"As women it is so often difficult for us to make space for our creative lives We prioritize our families, our homes, the business of day-to-day existence, and expect creative work to squeeze in at the margins. Barbara DeMarco-Barrett's wonderful, practical guide teaches us to value our craft and, thus, ourselves."

— Ayelet Waldman, author of *A Really Good Day*

"*Pen on Fire* soars with inspiration and crackles with joy. It's a blessing for anyone going crazy trying to find time to write."

— Carolyn See, author of *Making a Literary Life*

"The simple tips and easy lessons herein will provide inspiration to beginning and seasoned writers alike. I recommend it highly."

— Jo-Ann Mapson, *Owen's Daughter*

For Brian, Travis, and Dominique

"Only those who will risk going too far can
possibly find out how far one can go."

– T.S. Eliot

"You know how it is early in the morning on the water, and then
you come ashore, and in no time at all you're up to your ears in
trouble, and you don't know how it began."

– John Garfield, *Breaking Point*

I'm grateful to the editors of the journals and anthologies where these stories were first published: *Kelp Journal* and *Best of Kelp Journal* for Pushcart Prize nominee "Rowboat"; *Crossing Over* (Sisters in Crime San Diego) for "Pool Fishing"; *Orange County Noir* (Akashic) and *USA Noir: Best of the Akashic Noir Series* for "Crazy for You"; *Paradigm Shifts: Typewritten Tales of Digital Collapse* (Cold Hard Type) for "Hunting Season"; *Writing in Place: Stories from the Pandemic* (Mars Street Press) for "One's Company, Two's a Crowd"; *Literary Hatchet* for "51 Winfield," "Animals," and "Doors"; *Shotgun Honey* for "Noise"; SCWA *California Is a State of Mind* for "Making Peanuts at Pachanga"; *Rock and a Hard Place* for "Pink Aviary"; *Palm Springs Noir* (Akashic) for "The Water Holds You Still"; *Becoming Nosferatu: Stories Inspired by Silent German Horror* (BearManor Media) for "Sandman"; *Dark City Crime and Mystery Magazine* and *Coolest American Stories 2022* for "Blue Martini."

Details, story titles, and character names may vary from the originals. Revising never ends.

CONTENTS

THE WATER HOLDS YOU STILL

The landline rang after midnight. It had to be my mother down in Palm Springs. She was the only one, other than solicitors, who still called me on that line.

I picked up. "Hi, Mom."

"I heard a noise," she said.

I stood my brush in a jar of water. Red paint escaped the bristles, a blood cloud. I took the phone outside, the curly black cord stretched taut as a tightrope. Ferns along the patio beaded up with night mist, common here in coastal Orange County.

"Houses settle at night and make noises," I said.

A few months ago, she began calling me about noises at night, and the calls came more often.

A puff of breath and the faint strain of music—Sinatra. "Mood Indigo." She'd become obsessed with him, more so since my stepfather, Jerry, died.

"A coyote was outside by the pool, sniffing the water."

"Maybe it's bored," I said. "No little dogs around to eat."

"Greta, that's not funny," she said.

"You're keeping Joey Bishop in, right?" She loved red Pomeranians. When one died, she adopted another.

"He's in." Her voice dropped an octave. "My sapphire ring is missing. Every time your brother stops by, something else goes missing."

"Are you sure?" Out on Pacific Coast Highway, red and blue lights whirled by.

"Last week it was my diamond earrings. I planned to give those to you."

I took it personally. My brother knew I had dibs on those. "Has anyone other than Ben been around?"

"Repair people. Pool cleaner. Gardener. I can't keep track."

"So, it could be anyone."

"Do you think your brother's gambling again?" she asked. "People go to those pawn shops up on Palm Canyon and over in Cathedral City to sell things they steal. Or they sell them on Clubslist."

"You mean Craigslist."

"Make fun."

"Look, Mom," I said. "If Ben's stealing from you, call the police. Turn him in."

"I can't. He's my son."

"It will only get worse." I feared for my mother, brother, and me. Families weren't supposed to be like this. Sons didn't steal from their mothers. She'd complained before, so there must have been some truth to his thieving. "You'd be doing him a favor."

"He won't come and see me. Then who will I have?"

"You have me." I felt like that little girl again, competing with my brother for her love. Ours was a complicated relationship. Mothers and daughters and sons—oh my. She had that old-world Italian thing going: sons were gods; daughters were—what?

"You're so far away," she said.

"I'm not that far away, only a couple hours. Come stay with me for a while. There's a pool here. It's not like your pool, but it's something."

"I don't drive anymore. My eyes."

"Then I'll come there."

We made plans for me to drive to the desert in three days and hung up. Back in the studio, I studied my many unfinished canvases propped against the walls. I'd never get another gallery show if I didn't finish already. I had done well at my first show, but how could it ever happen like that again? What if I became a one-hit wonder? And was that better than becoming a follow-up failure? When Andrew and I broke up—I found out via Instagram, of all things, he'd cheated on me with an ex-girlfriend—my confidence plummeted. Faulty female intuition. The dickhead. I lost my motivation, and my creative ideas turned to mush.

By Friday morning, I'd made little progress on my painting, but I had to visit my mother.

I threw a few things into a suitcase—changes of clothes, sarong, bathing suit—bagged a bottle of wine, got into my MINI and headed east, Amy Winehouse crooning "Back to Black."

Past Redlands on Interstate 10, the land yawned open. The hills were curvy, a smooth velveteen. A freight train passed alongside the freeway. Blades of wind generators spun.

I took the exit for Highway 111, and ten minutes later the lunar landscape gave way to Palm Springs's green lawns and lush landscaping fed by a humongous underground lake.

Palm Canyon Drive runs through downtown, and even though it was August, pedestrians milled about. The desert city no longer cleared out during the searing summer months. I liked it better back when tumbleweeds rolled down the streets as the theme song from *The Good, The Bad, and The Ugly* played in my head.

At the stoplight near Rocky's Pawn Shop I called my brother and left a voicemail. Just beyond the Ace Hotel I hung a right and turned into Twin Palms, named for the two palm trees the developers planted in front of each mid-century marvel. My father bought one of the original homes, and Mom lived here through three husbands. I pulled into the curving driveway and made a mental note to ask about her car.

From the outside, the house looked the same: the butterfly design—sleek angular lines spread open like wings, high windows with broad panes of glass, chartreuse front door.

As I made my way up the front walk, things began to look awry. Empty vegetable and dog food cans littered either side of the cement path as if someone had pitched them out the front door instead of into the trash. And why hadn't Ben picked them up? Was he losing it too?

I rang the doorbell. Through the walls, a vague chime. I shifted from foot to foot, knocking, ringing the doorbell, and waiting. It took a while for my mother to respond, and when she did, she opened the door a crack.

"Who are you?" she said, peering out.

"I'm your daughter, remember me?" I said, indignant, though I freaked out inside.

"You look different." She let me in.

"I cut my hair." I reached up, touched the ends dyed blue.

"Why'd you do that?"

My hair was long until last month when I kicked out Little Dick.

"I needed a change," I said.

"What the hell is with the turquoise?"

I dropped my bags in my old bedroom, which looked the same since my last time here, put the wine in the fridge, and joined her in the kitchen. Joey Bishop spun as he barked. Yappy dogs can drive you right over the edge. Maybe this happened to her; it was the dog's fault. I leaned down to pet his head. He growled and snapped at me. I jumped back.

"He's very protective," she said.

"Not from your son, apparently," I mumbled.

"What did you say?"

"Oh, nothing."

The inside of the house was in better shape than the front walk, but something felt off. The big plate glass windows were smudged at the bottom from Joey Bishop's snout. Big antiques were missing—the carved Chinese table my father bought in my twelfth year. A bronze mirror that hung opposite the front door, supposedly from the Tang dynasty. Then there were the missing Eames coffee table and Slim Aarons photographs.

End tables and built-in shelves were bare of artifacts collected over the years from her trips to Europe and Asia, and the wood was dusty, except for circles and squares that were varying levels of clean, the chalk outline equivalent of missing items.

A yellowing pile of *Desert Sun* newspapers as tall as a toddler stood by the sliders.

I ran my fingers up the side. "You going to read all these?"

"I'll get to them," she said, and shuffled to her mid-century stereo cabinet. Hanging on the wall behind it were dozens of framed photos, mostly of Ben and me, but also of the Palm Springs celeb set she once hung out with. She set down the needle of the turntable on vinyl. Sinatra again, singing "In the Wee Small Hours of the Morning" from his saddest album.

I poured wine into a mug with the Marilyn Monroe flying skirt image. After that long drive, I deserved a drink. It was five o'clock somewhere, right? I took my cup and wandered about the house, noting all that was missing or just plain wrong. I threw away an empty plastic milk carton on the floor by her nightstand. On the wall where a Slim Aarons photo once hung, the paint appeared a shade lighter.

"Where is it?" I asked, pointing.

"Where is what?"

"My favorite photo of the Kaufmann house."

"That's been gone a long time."

"It was here the last time I visited. Four months."

"Seems like longer," she said. "Ask your brother."

"When does Ben come by? His voicemail is full."

"He comes over every night to swim," she says. "His new religion. What do you want for dinner?"

She threw open the fridge to reveal a dismal collection of milk, condiments, wilted iceberg lettuce, and not much else.

"Let's go to the store," I said.

"You go." She handed me her checkbook. "Take one, unless you need more."

"You shouldn't be handing out checks like Halloween candy."

"You're my daughter," she said. "If I can't trust you, who can I trust?"

"Do you say the same thing to Ben?"

"He's my son," she said.

When I returned with groceries, I set the bags on the bench outside the front door, picked up the tin cans and threw them out, and carried the bags inside. Mom sat on the sofa paging through a *Palm Springs Life*. Out by the pool, the first man in a long time who intrigued me skimmed the water with a long-poled net, sweeping leaves, bugs, and crud into it. He wore khaki board shorts, a neon yellow rash guard like what a surfer wears, and a wide-brimmed straw hat. He looked to be pure muscle, calves striated like rocks carved by river currents. He moved to his own soundtrack and swished the pool sifter back and forth. Such a gorgeous pool, a far cry from the one where I lived, not to mention the pool cleaner.

"That's Ernesto," my mother said without looking up from the magazine.

I put away the frozen foods and went out to introduce myself.

Tall, with eyes the color of kiwi fruit, he said he'd tended the pool three times a week for the last two months.

"That's a lot, isn't it?" I said.

"It's what the man wants," he said.

"What man? My brother?"

"Ben he said his name was."

So the house can go to hell but the pool needs to be pristine. Interesting.

"And you are?" he asked.

"Greta," I said. "It's nice to meet you. I'll leave you to your work." I turned toward the house.

"Que bonita," he said, perhaps to himself.

"Pardon?"

Rather shyly, he said, "You're much more beautiful than your picture."

I felt flustered, then dizzy, then smitten. It happened so fast, like I had just been hit with the flu. "How'd you see my photo?"

"Your mother asked me to look at her stereo. Sound would not come out. Your photos are on the wall."

"Do you want a drink?" I said. Was I hitting on him or had he just hit on me?

"A *cerveza* would be nice. So hot." He wiped a red bandana across his forehead.

"I don't think there's beer, but I'll check. I have wine."

"Whatever you like, I like," he said.

I stumbled on my way inside. *What was this?* I wanted him, and that he wanted me too might be enough to turn any whisper of an idea into a roar of demand.

I poured more wine into my mug and filled one that said PALM SPRINGS. Through the floor-to-ceiling windows that took up the entire back of the house, Ernesto scooped water from the pool into a vial and squeezed in a chemical. Capped the bottle, gave it a shake, then dipped in litmus paper. He looked young; his face and body were absent of history. When I was eighteen, I wanted a few wrinkles so I'd be taken more seriously. Imagine. Now, closer to forty than thirty, I lapped up his attention like a neglected kitten.

In my old room I changed into my two-piece. Dust bunnies hugged corners. This wasn't like my mother. She used to keep a pristine home, vacuumed and dusted as if cleaning were a full-time job.

"*Si, muy hermosa,*" he said, looking me up and down as I approached in my two-piece. I handed Ernesto a mug of wine. It wasn't like me to find a man I'd just met, my mother's pool cleaner at that, so instantly compelling. But after my lying, little-dick boyfriend—he'd even proposed!—I was game. I needed an ego boost, and fast.

Plus, this thing with Ernesto, whatever it was, would distract me from my growing concern over my mother and brother. A tryst while I was here would be sublime.

I laid a towel over the lounge chair and sat down. He took the chair beside me, and we made chitchat. He told me about his mother, a green-eyed blonde from L.A. who lost the part to Bo Derek in that awful movie, *Bolero,* but got a walk-on part and met his father, also an aspiring actor. I was only half listening; this gnawing animal attraction drew my attention.

How did he come to be a pool cleaner in Palm Springs?

"Time to leave L.A.," he said, and shook his head. He didn't offer more, and I didn't ask. I didn't care.

I must have been nervous because I downed that wine like a ginger shot. I jumped up, padded inside, and grabbed the bottle.

When I sat back down, I said, "I'm curious. Have you seen my brother doing anything strange?"

"Strange?"

"Things are missing from the house."

He pondered this and said, "One day I arrived as he put a black table into his car. He asked me for help."

"Was it carved?"

"With dragons," he said.

The Chinese table.

"Another time he carried out a cardboard box with pictures in frames."

That Slim Aarons print.

Ernesto's cellphone pinged with an incoming text. He looked at his phone and said, "Filter emergency."

I got up with him. He went to shake my hand, or maybe kiss it, when I pulled him into a hug.

"How old are you?" I said, looking for a reason to stay away from him.

"What's age?" He gave me his card with a graphic of a diving board and his contact info. "Call if you want to talk," he said, and with that, he pulled his trolley with bottles and hoses and disappeared through the side gate.

I went inside and changed. I vacuumed and cleaned the house. An hour later Ben showed up. My handsome little brother was losing his hair and had teeth in need of whitening strips. We side-hugged. I followed him outside. The sun had moved behind San Jacinto Peak, turning the sky a sulky violet.

He pulled a pack of cigarettes from his shirt pocket and offered me one. I shook my head. I'd stopped smoking and didn't want to start up again. My brother's hands trembled as he lit one for himself.

"I'm worried about Mom," I said. "She called the other night about a noise. She's getting worse."

"She has her good days and her bad days," he said, puffing away. The smoke hung in the windless air, our own personal smog alert. I hated wind, but right now I longed for it.

I waved away the smoke. "She says things are missing."

"Imagining things is a sign of early-stage dementia. What kinds of things?"

"Art. Jewelry. The dragon table—where is it?"

"What table? I didn't take a table. What am I going to do with a table?"

"It was worth a lot of money."

"Lots of people go in and out of the house," he said. "There's no telling. Old people are hungry for friends."

"That's bullshit."

"Is it?"

Ben set down the cigarette and pulled off his T-shirt.

"You're growing a belly there," I said.

He gave me the stink eye.

Three crows perched on the branch of a huge ficus tree, complaining about something or other.

He stamped out his cigarette, lit another, and offered me the pack. "Stop doing that," I said. "It took me forever to quit."

He shrugged. "Whatever."

"And the house is filthy," I said. "I found an empty milk carton beside her bed."

"She was probably thirsty."

I didn't laugh.

"You were supposed to look after her," I said. "Make sure she has food and a clean house."

"I am!"

"You're not doing a good job of it."

"Why don't you move back, then?" he said. "You can take care of all this crap."

The underwater lights of the pool came on. Ben went into the house, returned a few minutes later in his trunks, and dove in.

I stood to stretch. My mother stood on the other side of the slider, gazing out. I waved, but she made no gesture to show she saw me and evaporated back into the darkened house.

"What's up with all the darkness, Mom?" I stepped inside and slid the glass door shut behind me.

"The bulbs burned out." She wandered back over to the slider. "Your brother thinks he's a fish. Always swimming."

When we were kids, my brother and I swam as close to the bottom as we could, lay on our backs, and opened our eyes. Above, the water became a stained-glass window to the world. Once, as we surfaced, I pushed Ben back under and held him there, wishing, in a way, that he'd drown so I'd get back the attention he took from me when he came along. I still had nightmares about it, only in my dreams he sinks to the bottom and my father dives in to save him. I always woke up before they surfaced.

By the light of my phone, I searched the drawers for bulbs, replaced what I could, and switched them on. When all lit up, the house looked even dingier. I heated up a mac-and-cheese in the microwave, made a salad, and set plates on the table. Ben hefted himself out of the pool, dried off, and came in.

"Are you hungry?" asked our mother.

"Have an appointment." He kissed her on the cheek, gave a little wave to me, and said, "Good to see you," and scampered down the hallway and out the front door.

"Your brother always has meetings."

"At night?"

"He's a very busy man."

She got up. I heard the bathroom door close. When she returned, she said, "I can't find my ruby ring. I keep it in the bathroom drawer."

"What's it doing in the bathroom?"

"That's where I keep it."

I went to look, riffled through her vanity drawers, and found it, wrapped in a tissue.

"Here." I placed it in front of her plate.

She picked it up and held it close to her eyes. "Where was it?"

"In the bathroom." Hard to know what she imagined and what was real.

I filled my mug, but I needed more than wine. I needed Ernesto.

"C'mon, Mom, you have to eat."

She took a bite. "He was such a sweet boy. I used to dress him in the cutest outfits." A bemused expression skittered across her face. "So smart."

What I remembered was a smart-ass kid who always tattled on me, who pulled scary pranks, and who once almost got me killed at a busy intersection when we were on our bikes.

I tonged salad onto our plates.

"He must be gambling," she said. "What else would he do with the money I withdraw from the bank?"

"The bank?"

"Sometimes we go to the bank so I can take out money. Last week it was two thousand. What does he do with it?"

"Dollars?"

"He says we need things. Repairs." She gestured. "House is old."

There goes my inheritance.

"I meant to ask: where's your car?"

She shrugged. "Ask your brother."

"Oh my God," I said. "He doesn't tell me anything useful and neither do you."

She pushed back her chair, wandered over to the windows, and gazed out at the pool flashing blue in the darkness. "We used to have such parties. Frank would come by. He had a house a few streets over. This was before he married Barbara. Do you remember him? You were just a little girl. He'd come over, and we'd sit by the pool and drink Jack Daniel's. That was his drink, you know. He was a very nice man, always nice to you. I have all his albums. He gave them to me."

I did remember Sinatra, how he would sing in our living room, all my mother's friends gathered around.

She sighed. "I'm going to bed." Before she disappeared around the corner, she said, "Where does the time go?"

I'd begun to wonder the same thing myself.

Slippers scuffed down the hallway, followed by Joey Bishop's nails slipping across the floor. Her bedroom door clicked shut. I held Ernesto's business card, kept turning it over in my hands, and finally gave in. I texted him, asked what he was doing. Watching TV, he said. Come over, I said. He lived the next town over in Cathedral City and could be here in half an hour.

I cleaned the kitchen and paged through a newspaper that had fallen from the stack. A feature about the growing crime of elder abuse in the desert, prevalent because of the older people here with property and money.

I didn't want to believe that's what Ben was doing. But somebody was doing something nefarious.

Such a sweet boy.

When did sweet turn to sour?

I flipped through the paper. Buried on page five was a story about a pool drowning from electric shock. A lot of swimming pools in Palm Springs were built before 1963 and not all were up to code. Who even knew to get the wiring of their pools checked twice a year?

I called my brother. He picked up.

"What did you do with Mom's car?" I asked.

"Look," he said. "You're not around. You don't know what goes on here."

"Enlighten me, then: what goes on here?"

"She's losing it," he said.

"Today you said she has her good days and her bad days."

"You're afraid for your inheritance, aren't you? I'm the one who deserves payback. You left. You don't care about Mom."

"Screw you," I said, and hung up. My face felt hot. I found a bottle of tequila in the liquor cabinet, probably five years old from when Jerry was still alive—maybe from their last cocktail party—and set it on the counter. There was a faint rap on the slider. A silhouette of a man framed against the turquoise of the pool. I jumped.

Ernesto.

"You scared me," I said, hand on heart, sliding open the door.

"I have a key for the gate."

I held up the bottle. "Look what I found. I'll pour us some over ice."

We took our tumblers out to the pool along with the half-full bottle and sat side by side on lounge chairs.

"I thought about you today," he said.

"What did you think?"

"You in that bikini." He tapped his forehead. "It's right here."

"I thought of you, too." Tequila wended its way through me, tamping down the circuits, loosening the boundaries between me and everything else.

He took hold of my hand and gave it a tug.

"Come sit," he said. I snuggled into him on the lounge chair as if I'd known him forever. He stroked my arm, then my shoulder, trailed his fingers over the cliff of my clavicle and kept traveling south under my tank top. He gave my chest a delicious massage.

"You have some hands on you," I said.

"That's not all I have," he said, which is when he tugged at the waistband of my shorts, and I let him. I pulled them off, pulled his off. We had sex by my mother's pool under the stars as bats fluttered among the palm fronds.

Afterward we jumped in the pool to rinse off, wrapped ourselves in towels, and went back to the lounge chairs. I poured more tequila. We toasted to us.

I awoke as the sun inched up over Indian Canyons. On the other side of the pool a coyote sniffed the water. I clapped my hands, and he jumped over the gate and ran.

Inside, my mother was still asleep. After a shower, I knotted a sarong at my waist, brewed a pot of coffee, and checked my cellphone. A message from my brother.

"I don't appreciate being hung up on—"

Delete.

Another message, this one from Little Dick. "Greta, I keep telling you, I'm sorry. It was a mistake. I meant it when I said I want to marry you."

Delete.

Screw them. Screw both of them.

My brother continued to come over every night to swim—usually at sundown when my mother went to bed. We ignored each other. My mother was the same, ignoring me but vaguely glad I was here.

Right after Ben left, I'd text Ernesto. He'd come over and we'd have sex, and then we'd talk. Mostly I talked. Over the next few nights, I told him the long story of my past with Little Dick, my painting, why I was here. Admittedly, I'd grown addicted to his silky fingers that made my body feel things it hadn't felt in years.

It was bugging me, what my mother said about going to the bank. I wondered if I'd find out anything if I went through her expandable file.

I found papers for a reverse mortgage. What the hell? I about exploded out of my sarong.

My mother was in the garage, going through a box of old photos.

"Why'd you take out a reverse mortgage on the house?" I asked.

Studying a faded color photo, she said, "Ben said I should spend the money before I croak."

"But what do you need it for?"

"I don't need it but just in case."

"Unbelievable." I returned to the file and the bank statements and a huge headache that two Advil and a glass of wine helped to mute.

That night as Ernesto and I lay naked in the balmy night air, I said, "I have to do something, go to court, get power of attorney or something so my brother doesn't take all my mother's assets."

"Court takes a long time, no?"

"By the time it goes through, my mother could be penniless. Already fifty grand is gone."

"How much is left?"

"Around a hundred grand. Probably more."

"Still, a lot of money," he said.

We watched the glimmery blue water, listened to the mockingbird that ran through its repertoire of cellphone ringtones, and sipped tequila. My eyes fixed on the underwater light.

I brought up the article. "I've read that a lot of pools here are not code compliant. Old pools, old wires." I paused before asking, "Is it painful, drowning that way? Do you think it hurts?"

"The swimmer feels a tingling, becomes kind of numb, can't get out, gets sucked under."

"My brother swims all the time," I said.

"I check pools to make sure this does not happen."

A shiver ran through me when I realized what I was thinking. I wanted my brother gone, and I needed Ernesto's help to make it happen. There was a name for that, and it wasn't good.

The next evening when Ben came over, he brought Mom a cherry pie, her favorite, and exclaimed for the universe to hear that he hired a cleaning lady.

He went out to swim laps and Mom went to bed. I stood over the glistening pool.

"I know what you're doing," I said.

He pretended he didn't hear. Water in his ears or something.

"You don't fool me," I continued, and sat on a lounge chair with my drink, hoping to intimidate him into leaving. I watched him swim back and forth—not for much longer, though, if things went as planned. I used to like my brother more, even love him, but for years he was all about Ben, and I'd had my fill.

That night Ernesto and I went at it in our usual place, on the lounge chair beside the pool. Thank God for mothers who go to bed early and for magenta bougainvillea that grows tall along stucco walls surrounding properties. Sex with Ernesto was good for my nerves—better than any painkiller. This thing with my brother had my nerves sheared raw.

We rinsed off in the pool then sat on the bullnose edge, sipping tequila.

"I'd be willing to give you some of the money."

"Excuse me?" he said.

"The last straw was the reverse mortgage. He needs to pay for what he did. You can help me, can't you?"

He took a big sip. "Oh, *chica*, this can be very dangerous."

"It's a lot of money, you even said that."

"I know, but I—"

"You know how to make pools safe, right? So, you must know what makes them unsafe."

"I can't disconnect anything, but I can do something, make the wiring look frayed maybe."

"No one will ever know you had anything to do with it. I'd never tell them how to find you. Why would I?"

I ran my hand over his lower regions. "I would do anything to show my appreciation for your efforts on my behalf," I said, and we went at it again.

Afterward I said, "I need a picture of us," and reached for my phone.

"Oh, no," he said. "I don't like to take pictures."

I leaned my face against his, anyway, reached out my arm, and took a selfie. My breasts and his bare chest were in the shot. So sexy. A photo to keep me company when he wasn't around.

"I've never met anyone like you," he said as I licked a bead of sweat from his cheek.

"There's more of this for you, whenever you like," I said.

He shook his head and kissed me hard. "Tomorrow I'll come over and play with the wires. Just don't forget and jump in the water yourself."

My brother fetched my mother for breakfast, just the two of them. I did errands. When I returned, I dodged yappy Joey Bishop—maybe he'd get dizzy and faint from spinning as he barked—and stood before the pool. It looked so pristine, so innocent. I dropped in a palm frond to see what would happen. It did not sizzle. It did not fry. I wasn't going to jump in to test the water. Hopefully Ernesto had been here and done his thing.

I was in the bathroom slathering on sunblock when Mom returned. She shuffled down the hallway, followed by her frantic little pooch. "I'm going to rest," she said.

I called after her. "Where's Ben?"

"Had to work." She closed her door.

Work. What work?

When the sky turned lavender, the pool lights came on. I poured a drink and heard the front door.

Ben was here, using his key, striding through the house like he owned it, heading for the pool. I purposely didn't turn on lights in the living room so I could watch him.

The desert wind stirred up fronds and dust, sweeping them against the house and into the pool. The south end of town rarely got hit hard, but this evening the wind was wicked and sent a standing umbrella onto its side, missing Ben by inches. He jumped out of its way, then picked it up and leaned it against the stucco wall.

My mother's bedroom door creaked open. Out scampered Joey Bishop, who sniffed my feet, barked, and ran out the open slider toward the pool.

"Don't!" I called. He trotted back, spinning as he barked.

My mother stood beside me and watched my brother standing by the water. The room was freezing; she must have turned the air down to sixty-five.

"We saw Ernesto at breakfast," she said.

"Who?" I played dumb.

"Your *boyfriend*," she said. So, she'd seen me with him. "Ben took me to Cathedral City, some little restaurant. Your boyfriend was there, with his wife and kids."

My brother dove in, began swimming laps.

I felt hot all over. "How do you know they were his wife and kids?"

"They called him Daddy."

Ben slowed and seemed to struggle, as if an invisible force pulled at him.

"Why isn't he moving?" Her voice quavered.

"Maybe he has a cramp."

I felt awful. A mother shouldn't have to watch her son die.

"Call 9-1-1!" She flailed her hands about like startled birds. I found my phone and called.

Ben gestured toward the house for help, then stopped struggling and was sucked under. He rose to the surface and lay inert on the water.

The sirens grew close and then the paramedics were here. I let them in and said, the way a frantic person would, "My brother! He's in the pool!" and three men rushed past. Joey Bishop spun like a top out of control, barking till he went hoarse.

I followed them out.

"Does your brother know how to swim, ma'am?"

"Of course!"

"Does he take drugs?"

"I don't know! He comes over every night to swim."

They mumbled among themselves, then one of them went over and unplugged the wiring and filter and whatever else was electrical. The other two used the leaf skimmer and a rope to pull his limp body from the pool. They administered CPR, but Ben wasn't responding.

The carved dragon table, the Slim Aarons photos. Ernesto, with a wife and kids? The world was full of rats.

As they tried CPR on my brother, I rushed inside. I would give them Ernesto's business card, give Ernesto to them. Mom sat in the dark of the living room while there was Sinatra again, singing about a piper man and losing someone to the summer wind. But as I held the card, I realized that by giving them Ernesto, I would also be giving them me.

I went back outside. They were loading Ben onto a stretcher. His cigarettes lay on a chair. Oh, what the hell. I grabbed them, tapped one from the pack, and lit up. On my phone I looked at the picture of Ernesto and me. Gave me pangs to think it was over. I flicked the card against the phone, then the thought came to me: maybe his wife would like the photo, too.

BLUE MARTINI

I wanted to be alone. I wanted to be far away. Because every night and every day, Gunther and I fought about stupid things. He always had to have the last word. So did I. Not a great combination. A couple like us couldn't last. The fight we most often had was over the bills. Since he paid all the bills, he wanted me to help him with his new business. Like hell, I said. I wasn't going to get involved with crystal meth no matter what. It rots your brain, I told him. It makes you dull inside. He didn't like that, and the last time I said it, he squeezed my arms so hard he polka-dotted my skin red and made me yelp.

After that, we kept our distance more than usual, which was fine with me. He'd stay out in the RV creating his *Breaking Bad* concoction, as he liked to call it. If Walter White could get rich manufacturing crystal, so could he. "You idiot," I finally said, "it's a TV show," and this set off some major league arguing. Gunther had a degree in chemistry, and, like Walter White, he thought he would use his education to make real money. He deserved to have a good life, he claimed more than once. You call this good? I wanted to shout this time, but now, as our voices rose yet again, I tried to fight fair by merely saying, "Walter White was a fictional antihero."

He wanted me to explain "antihero." See, that's what I was dealing with. He was a brilliant chemist but an idiot about everything else.

The bigger idiot for sticking around so long—almost a year—was me. I had a front-row seat watching my boyfriend transform from one handsome dude into a skinny, crank-addled asshole. Don't let anybody tell you differently—speed turns you ugly, makes you sell out your mother, your grandmother, your best friend. After I explained that an antihero was what he saw when he looked in the mirror, he stormed off and sought refuge in his ugly-ass RV. I'd had enough.

No telling if he would be out in that thing for thirty minutes or three hours, so I hurried. I packed the car my mother left me when she died last year, my thirty-third birthday gift, a rusted white '78 Cadillac Eldorado with red leather seats, red carpeting, a red steering wheel, and a plastic hula girl on the dashboard. I loved that car but would rather have my mother back.

Also from my mother was a set of pink Samsonite suitcases. One I stuffed with clothes. In the other went my baking tools—rolling pin, hand mixer, pie plate. I was all set to go when I jogged back to the house and grabbed the half-full bottle of tequila from the liquor cabinet and one of Gunther's many guns, a .32-caliber pocket pistol, one he jokingly said he won from a woman in a game of strip poker. It was a tiny thing with an ivory grip and silver plating, a fancy toy he said was suitable for me because it would fit in my pocketbook.

"It's a purse," I told him. "No one calls it a pocketbook anymore."

I also couldn't forget Tomasina, a jar of sourdough starter named for my mother who gave it to me before I left Costa Mesa to be with Gunther. I was intent on returning to the beach city of my childhood. My cousin had a two-bedroom apartment in a little '50s-style converted motel. She said I could have one of the rooms.

I scribbled, "Have a good life. Fuck you—" on an envelope and left it under Gunther's stained coffee cup. Outside, the heat felt like somebody forgot to turn off the oven, and let's not forget the smell—good riddance to the rotten egg fumes from the Salton Sea a few miles south.

Before I took off, I checked out my reflection in the rearview. "You are one sad fuck," I said to the gray eyes that looked back. "Get it together."

My white-and-red land yacht lurched onto the rutted macadam. West of me, the sun was making a break for the San Jacinto Mountains, which carved a jagged line in the empty blue sky. Out here on the edge of the Coachella Valley, an hour from Palm Springs, secondary road care wasn't on the city's list of priorities. I pulled onto the shoulder beside a family of prickly pear cacti and turned off the GPS on my cell. The land yacht had been handling the bumps in the road okay, but something sounded off. Every so often the engine emitted the tiniest of hiccups. I refused to worry; freedom was at hand. I forged ahead, turned onto the 111, and headed south. If the traffic was with me, I'd be at my cousin's in three hours tops. On the car radio, I tuned in a desert station and landed on Sam Cooke's "You Send Me."

My mother, sister, and I loved Sam Cooke. When this song would come on with the three of us in this car, we'd sing along, a regular trio girl band. I turned up the radio and sang backup about someone Cooke loved so much. I couldn't remember anyone other than my mother loving me that much. But as she said, it ain't over till the fat lady sings. Opera isn't the same as life, I'd tell her, but she laughed and told me not to take things so literally.

Instead of getting on the 10 West with a clear shot to the ocean, I stayed on the 111 and made a stop in Palm Springs for a late lunch: veggie sandwich and an Arnold Palmer at Sherman's Deli. Lining the back wall were signed black and white headshots of stars who used to hang out in Palm Springs—Sinatra, Dean Martin, Rita Hayworth. Old Hollywood. When Gunther and I were first together, before his current business took off and while he still had meals, we would drive into Palm Springs for dinner. It was different being here alone, but I didn't mind. I liked my own company. At an outside table on the patio, misters spritzed fine spokes of water that moistened my arms and made the heat bearable.

I eavesdropped on the conversations around me.

Let's do the Thursday night art walk.

Where can we find Drag Queen Bingo?

Does that Desert Oracle podcast dude still do a show at the Ace?

Let's go to Mr. G's for a puzzle. Thousand piecer.

People were planning their todays, looking forward to their tomorrows. I envied the lot of them. I wanted a tomorrow to look forward to. I had a hundred bucks to my name and a credit card that Gunther would soon shut down. I charged my lunch and left a 50 percent tip. Why not? Gunther's parting gift to me.

Back in the Caddy, I set a bag of sugar cookies for my cousin on the red leather seat, stuck my key in the ignition, and turned. *Clickety-click.*

Damn it.

When I first met Gunther, he repaired fancy cars. With that brain of his, he could figure out any engine. He once offered to teach me the world under the hood, but I was too worried about my fucking manicure.

The engine could be flooded. That much I knew. I waited a moment and tried again. A click no louder than a lizard's toenail against stone.

I wrangled open the hood, leaned over the engine, and peered in as if I knew what to look for. Dirt from the Caddy's monstrous grille frosted the front of my white jeans and top with an outline of what looked like a giant charcoal mouth laughing at me. Great. Just great.

An older dude ambled over, hands in blue jeans, loose white short-sleeve shirt, blue-billed cap that said *Singleton Landscapes* in yellow, his faded blond hair curling out from it. Eyes swimming-pool green. A Robert Redford lookalike. Grizzled, and still hot.

"What's the problem?" he said. Southern twang. White teeth.

"It won't start," I said.

He grimaced in shared pain. "Let me have a look."

I moved aside, and he fiddled.

"Try firing her up."

I turned the key. Zilch.

He played around with the battery connections. "Got Triple A?"

I shook my head. Gunther had never wanted to pay for that, always said he could fix whatever needed fixing.

"I have cables," he said. "Hang on."

He jogged over to a pickup with *Singleton Landscapes* on its side doors and pulled the truck alongside the land yacht. Dug around in the truck bed, found a wreath of yellow and red cables, connected his battery to mine.

"Try it now."

This time the engine turned over. My chest expanded with relief. I'd be able to get out of the Coachella Valley today and far away from Gunther and my old, parched life.

He unhooked the cables and tossed them back in his truck. "That battery looks a mite old," he said. "You need a new one. If I was you, I'd get a battery before you get back on the road."

I thanked him, and, as he remained watching, I slid behind the steering wheel, revved the motor, and the engine died again. He squinted down the street as if he were looking for something.

"There's a shop just down a ways where a buddy works on vintage cars. My guess is your problem is more than the battery. Let's try jumping it again."

We did, and it stayed running. "Follow me," he said.

At first, I hesitated, but I didn't get weird vibes from him and serial killers tended to be younger, so I followed him a few blocks down Tahquitz to the shop. He introduced me to a guy in blue overalls with a white-and-blue embroidered name tag that said "Jeb." As he chewed a toothpick, Jeb connected the Caddy to a shiny red machine with lots of knobs, outlets, and wires.

"Your alternator's shot," Jeb said, wiping his hands on a blue rag. "It'll take a day or two to get the part. Alternators for these old cars are hard to find. Come by in the morning. I'll know more then."

"How much will it cost?" I asked.

He withdrew the toothpick, looked at it, then at my car. "Seven hundred at least, with labor."

By the time it would be ready, Gunther would likely have cut off my credit card.

Still, I told Jeb, "Okay."

Outside the shop, my rescuer held out his hand and said, "Billy Singleton. And you are?"

"Pepper Shannon."

"Glad to make your acquaintance, Pepper Shannon. You got a place to stay in town?"

"My cousin has friends not too far from here. I'll give her a call."

With his chin he pointed at the adjacent motel. "I know the owner. I can try to get you a deal."

I must have had doubt written all over my face, because he added, "Don't worry. No strings."

"All right. I'd greatly appreciate a deal."

"This way," he said, and I followed him across the dusty gravel lot to a one-story, blue clapboard motel with six units, seven if you counted the manager's quarters, and a little connected bar that looked closed. An unlit neon sign that said BLUE MARTINI along with a giant martini glass with an olive reached into the sky.

At the front desk Billy introduced me to the owner, Tanya, who had a turquoise brush cut and a tiny stud piercing her left nostril. He helped me with my suitcases. We strolled past the pool to the door of my room. He set the suitcase just inside the door and went to leave.

"Wait," I said. "Shot of tequila as a token of thanks?" I pulled the bottle from my tote bag.

"The holy cactus. Don't mind if I do." His face lit up with a bashful smile.

"Think there's an ice machine?"

He pointed inside the room at the Styrofoam bucket beneath the TV. "Wherever there's an ice bucket, there's gotta be ice." He took the bucket and disappeared into the twilight.

I looked at my phone. Three texts from Gunther. The other times I left him, he always talked me into coming back. Not this time. I turned up the swamp cooler that rattled and spewed tepid air. I found two plastic cups in the bathroom wrapped in sanitized paper coverings.

Billy returned with a bucket full of ice and filled our cups to the brim. I poured tequila and enjoyed the crackle of the ice as the alcohol hit. We toasted and drank. The tequila warmed me from my head down to my pinkie toes. My future took on a cheerful gleam. Maybe I'd been worrying for nothing. But I was sweating like a pig. I was used to air-conditioning at Gunther's. Billy took an ice shard and ran it down the side of my face and neck, stopping at my clavicle.

"How's that feel?" he said, his voice low and raspy.

He could tame scorpions with that voice.

"Very nice," I heard myself saying.

"C'mon." He took my hand and tugged me outside. "The magical hour betwixt darkness and light."

"A poet," I said.

"Just need to open our eyes. Beauty all 'round."

The violet sky did feel magical. The only times Gunther went outside anymore was when he had to go from the house to the RV or to the store. I'd become like a housebound binge-watching little housewife, me. How had it happened that I'd become immune to boring days on end?

Sinatra played through outdoor speakers. We wandered over to the swimming pool. Billy pulled me to him, and we slow danced. We sat on the bullnose edge of the pool and drank some more. He had such perfect arms, like those of a much younger man. Toned most likely from his work. Arms had never been such a turn-on. I wanted like anything to see what was under his shirt, but it was too soon.

I jumped up, fetched the tequila, and drained the bottle into our cups. We toasted, lay back on the cement, watched the night sky. Specks of stars poked through a blanket of indigo. We had the place to ourselves. By the time we finished drinking, the time was not only right, it was perfect. He switched off the pool light, and we peeled off our clothes, then jumped into the water, where we mated like seals who'd been beached too long.

I invited him to stay the night. We watched the motel TV and laughed at Jimmy Kimmel's monologue. It was like we'd known each other forever.

In the morning, the sun through the skimpy curtains woke us up. Eight more texts from Gunther. We drank coffee-maker coffee in bed.

"What the hell." Billy held one of my arms Gunther had squeezed too hard. The splotches had turned purple. I pulled away.

"How'd you get those?"

"Ran into a wall."

He shook his head and scowled. "That wall had some hands, did it?"

"I don't want to talk about Gunther."

"Gunther," he repeated, looking like he'd just tasted rancid food.

He stayed on simmer for a while, deliberating before he spoke. "That's one thing I can't tolerate, dudes who hurt women.

My brother-in-law put my sister in the hospital. And when they released her, she went back to him like nothing ever happened."

"Maybe she needed him to survive financially."

"She was a principal of a high school. Made far more money than that bastard."

"My mom had similar troubles, but she wasn't educated. Needed my dad for money."

"Money or no money," he said, "why don't women leave? They just stay and stay, as if saying 'more, more.'"

"It's not that they don't want to," I said. "Maybe they don't know how to, or they're afraid."

He ran his fingers across my bruises. Leaned over and kissed them. "I'd never do that to you. I'd shoot myself first. Does Gunther know where you are?"

"I can't see how he would."

"GPS on your phone?"

"Turned it off."

"Smart lady."

In the tiny shower stall, we soaped each other's torsos and backs, took turns under the showerhead to rinse, and toweled off. After we dressed, I said, "Want to go with me to see if Jeb found the part?"

"Whatever you want to do," Billy said.

The service bay smelled of oil and gasoline. On the radio, an angry talk show host blathered words: "socialist agenda," "family values." If I never heard the words "family values" again, it would be too soon.

"I found you an alternator," Jeb said, a toothpick lodged in the side of his mouth. "But it's going to take a few days, and, like I thought, it ain't gonna be cheap. Those old vintage parts . . ." His voice trailed off, but I did hear the words "alternator," "fuel pump," and "expensive."

"Can I think a minute?" I asked.

Jeb swiped a red licorice whip from a big plastic jar and replaced the toothpick with it. "Take all the time you need." Probably used to be a cigarette smoker and had that oral thing going on.

I considered asking my cousin for a loan. I stared at the fan belts hanging on the wall.

Jeb said to Billy, "What's happening with the bar? Looked closed last night."

"Tanya fired the bunch of 'em. They were stealing from her. She's hiring. Just put an ad on Craigslist."

"I could use a job," I interrupted. "Pay my repair bill, get me to Orange County. I could give you payments."

Billy and Jeb looked at me.

"That's a shittin' good idea," Billy said. "Let's talk to Tanya."

That night I started work behind the bar. I'd get to my cousin's in Costa Mesa when I got there. Making money was my number one priority. The Blue Martini was small. Knotty pine, six stools, three booths—that was it. Little neon beer signs, a large jar holding dill pickles in a filmy broth. Old time jukebox. Two vending machines, one with M&Ms, the other with peanuts. Basic liquors, well drinks, beer. Nothing too exotic except for the signature drink, a blue martini made with vodka, blue Curaçao, and triple sec.

At dusk, the place filled up. It was exciting, making money of my own again.

A litany of texts from Gunther kicked into high gear. I responded only once to say, *Leave me alone. Never coming home.*

At the end of my first week, with my paycheck and tips, I had almost half of what I needed to pay Jeb.

Into my second week, Billy stopped by just before closing, as he did every night. He took a stool at the end of the bar. Ordered a Corona. He looked as happy to see me as I was to see him. Whatever we had brewing hadn't grown old yet, and I hoped it never would. Some things were just meant to be.

"Listen, your ex visited Jeb." He slugged from the bottle.

"What?" My heart raced. "How'd he know my car was there?"

"That Caddy's unique. Maybe a buddy of his saw it in the garage's parking lot. The Coachella Valley's a small town."

"Would Jeb tell him I was working at the bar?"

Billy shook his head. "Doubt it."

A glass slipped from my grasp and shattered on the stone floor just beyond the bar floor mat. I spaced out on drink orders. Made a lemon drop martini when a cosmo was ordered, a margarita instead of a mojito. Billy stayed until the bar closed. I finished wiping down the counter and put away all the glasses.

"I'll walk you home," he said. "Make you feel better."

He did know how to make me feel good, forget about Gunther, and believe in new beginnings. A slight breeze swept over the San Jacinto, bringing with it cool mountain air. Billy set a brown paper bag on the little table. I filled cups with ice. He poured the tequila, and we drank. The moon was a big friendly face. The hissing of sprinklers watering lawns in the subdivision over the concrete brick wall serenaded us. A far cry from my life with Gunther.

"Why do they waste all that water on the desert?" I asked, more to the air than to Billy.

"People fancy green lawns."

"What's wrong with cacti?" I said. "I don't get it."

We soaked up the moon's rays and discussed driving up to Joshua Tree, where, Billy said, there were yuccas that looked like people praying. This was the life. I had a job and a dream of a man. Sure, he was older—much older—and I'd eventually be accused of having a daddy complex. Or he'd be called a cradle robber. I didn't care. Age was just a number.

Gunther was dissolving into the past, a nightmare I needed to forget. Billy and I sat out there for the longest time, and as had become our habit when it seemed no one would be leaving their rooms, we dropped our clothes and went for a swim.

The next morning, we went to Sherman's Deli for breakfast. I had a beignet that snowed powdered sugar all over me. We strolled Palm Canyon Drive like honeymooners, stopping in at Just Fabulous, where Billy bought me a pink flamingo pool floatie.

It was around ten o'clock that night when an RV with bull horns painted on the front pulled into the Blue Martini lot. There couldn't be two of those ugly-ass RVs around. Gunther.

Everyone in the bar was joshing it up to music on the jukebox. The lights of the RV went off. Every so often I went to the windows for a better view. The tiny spark of orange from his cigarette grew bright and faded, grew bright and faded. He was watching the bar, watching me. I wanted to get out of there, but I couldn't flake on Tanya. I was the only one on, and anyway, where would I go?

Around midnight Billy came in and took a seat at the bar. I placed a Corona before him.

"Sexy outfit," he said. "You were wearing that when we met."

"Took forever to get out the dirt from the car's grille."

"You look good enough to eat."

I leaned over and said, "Gunther found me."

Billy's face became a map of worry. "Where?"

"Don't look now, but that RV in the lot on your way in is his."

Billy pursed his lips and rubbed at a spot on the lacquered knotty pine as I slid my room key across the bar.

"I have his gun in the room," I said. "In the nightstand."

"Is it loaded?"

"I would assume."

"You don't know?"

"I didn't check. Maybe that's why he's here. Probably missed it after all."

"I doubt that's all he missed." Billy shut his eyes, gave a vague shake of his head, and got to his feet. "I'll unload it. You can give it back to the bastard so he leaves you alone. I brought my own gun, just in case." He reached down and tapped his ankle under his jeans.

"I didn't know you had a gun," I said.

"Who doesn't?"

He made a kissy face on his way toward the kitchen, and I made one too. Then I heard the kitchen screen door slap shut.

I carried on with the customers as if nothing was going on, as if it was a normal night. But there was nothing normal about Gunther.

Billy hadn't yet returned when Gunther came slinking in sloth-like.

"You shouldn't be here," I said.

"What time does this dive close? You're coming home with me. We'll fetch the Caddy tomorrow. Get me a beer."

"That's not my home," I said, and did not get him a beer.

"You know you love me." He cracked his knuckles. "What the hell is wrong with you?"

A couple of remaining diehards watched us from across the room.

"You're in love with meth," I said, "not me."

"Meth is why you get to sit on your ass all day and watch TV."

"I'm sick of TV. I need something to do. I'm doing it now."

"Tending bar? That's what you call doing something?"

I waved goodbye to the last customers, regulars who must've sensed trouble and didn't want to stick around for it. Gunther went to use the restroom. I poured the remains of a blue martini from a silver beaker into a cocktail glass and set it on the bar.

Billy was back. He lifted his T-shirt to show me the ivory and silver pistol in the waistline of his jeans.

"I left it loaded," he said.

"He's in the restroom." I wiggled my fingers.

"Jesus," he said. "Have you ever used a firearm?"

"Yes," I lied. If anything went wrong, I didn't want Billy going to jail. I would be the one.

"Hurry," I said, anxious. "He'll be back any second."

Billy handed over the gun though I could tell he didn't want to. I stuck it in the back of my jeans. So much love and concern poured from his eyes, so much warmth. I smiled, but he must have seen sadness or worry because he said, "You're the best woman I've ever known. Please be careful."

"Of course."

"Don't let the bastard get to you." He took a barstool.

Gunther returned and, as he approached, Billy rose from the stool, his chest pushed out, trying to look younger, stronger.

Gunther scowled. "You the new boyfriend?"

Billy looked down his beautiful nose at him.

Gunther turned to me and said, "You like old guys now, do you?" He licked his lips and clenched his jaw as he always did when he was high.

I wanted to spew forth a flurry of words, say how at least my old guy knew how to treat a lady. Instead, I folded my arms across my chest and said, "You need to go."

"No. *You* need to come home with me. You've been here long enough."

"Long enough for what? I'm never coming home."

"What the fuck, Pepper?"

Billy took a few steps toward Gunther. "Might be best if you left now."

Gunther glanced at Billy like he was an annoying elderly uncle. They were the same height. Billy was heavier, more filled out, but Gunther was lean and mean and fueled by meth. The pistol was cool against my back.

"Please go," I said. "It'd be better for everyone."

"What's better for everyone is for you to quit playing nursemaid to this old fool." He squeezed my shoulder so hard I felt bruises blossoming right then and there. I wrenched free. He grabbed my chin, forcing me to look at him. "I am not going to keep telling you. Time to come with me where you belong."

With a little push, he let go of my chin and my neck cracked, as if I'd just been chiropracted. Something about that crack and his once-handsome-now-gaunt pasty face made me snap. I whipped the gun from my waistband, held it with both hands, and pointed it at him.

He stepped back and raised his hands. "Put that toy away before you hurt yourself." He looked bemused.

"Get out." I wagged the gun at him.

"Pepper," Billy said.

"He needs to go," I said. "Now." My voice had a frantic edge, and it scared me.

"You won't use that on me," Gunther said. "You're too much of a fucking chicken."

That's when I squeezed the trigger, but as I did Gunther knocked my arm and the bullet missed him and hit Billy's shoulder. Billy fell backward, knocking the blue martini onto the floor, blue droplets splashing onto my white jeans. Billy whipped out his revolver and drilled Gunther in the chest. Gunter's face stayed brave, but he went down with an ugly moan. Etta James's "At Last" came on the jukebox.

Billy held his arm as I helped him up and over to a booth, where he said, "Like a nasty hornet sting is all."

"Oh, Billy." I ran to the bar, grabbed a clean bar towel, and rushed back to him.

I folded the white towel, pressed it against his wound, which was bleeding though not profusely. I'd gotten him on the side of the shoulder.

"Press," I said.

Billy nodded and bit down on his lip. I went over to Gunther, who lay there unmoving, and felt for a pulse. Nothing. He looked sweeter than I'd seen him in months. The old Gunther was back, the person he'd been before crystal turned him into a monster. Death, the ultimate relaxer, had loosened the ugly frown muscles of his face. I reached into his front pocket where he always kept a money clip. The metal felt cool on my fingers. There were at least twenty hundred-dollar bills. My severance pay for putting up with him for the last year. I checked his other pockets because sometimes, especially when he knew he'd be out of the house for a while, he kept backup cash in them. In these pockets I found thirty more C-notes.

I took Billy's gun, wiped it clean of prints.

"What are you doing?" he mumbled.

"I'm not letting you take the fall for this," I said. "Is it in your name?"

"No, ma'am."

"Good," I said.

I wrapped Gunther's fingers around the handle of the pistol so his prints would be on it. Then Billy took over, and I watched as he pointed Gunther's hand with the gun toward the opposite wall and fired. He shook Gunther's hand to make the gun fall. He did it calmly, carefully, as if this wasn't the first time.

Afterward, I called 9-1-1 and said, "There's been a shooting. One hurt, another maybe dead." The dispatcher asked for my name and the Blue Martini's address. When we hung up, I called Tanya, who said she'd be right over.

"You okay?" I called over to Billy, who gave me a weary thumbs-up. "They're going to question us," I continued. "Whatever you do, say Gunther threatened me."

"But he did," Billy said.

The sound of sirens grew louder, and then they were here, cop cars fishtailing into the gravelly lot, whirly lights throwing reds and blues on the walls and the ceiling of the Blue Martini. Firetrucks and paramedics followed. There were so many cruisers and emergency vehicles piling in, you'd think a carnival was taking place.

An EMT wheeled in a stretcher for Billy. I tilted the trash can for his blood-soaked bar towel. They loaded Gunther into another van.

Good riddance, I thought. Jackass.

I spent the night and most of the next day at the police station detailing what had happened. I claimed self-defense and gave the cops my history with Gunther. I told them about how I'd recently left him because he'd been going loco. I gave them the names of those last regulars who witnessed Gunther's aggression before they escaped into the night.

In the morning the police sent a car out to Gunther's house and another to the RV in the Blue Martini's lot.

One concerned cop, whose name was Glen Crookston, seemed to have it in for the meth dealers in the Valley, of which there were many. "They're turning this paradise into a sinkhole," he said.

My story about Gunther must have checked out, because it wasn't too long before this cop said I could go. A cruiser dropped me off at the Blue Martini. The RV was still there, wrapped in black-and-yellow caution tape.

I walked to my room and was there not even ten minutes when a cab pulled up and dropped off Billy. I ran out to meet him. His arm was in a sling and his shoulder looked bandaged.

"You're a sight for sore eyes," he said as I gave him a gentle side hug.

"Did they question you a lot?"

He lay back on the bed with a groan. "A fair amount."

"I'm worried. If they get forensics involved, I'm afraid our stories aren't going to check out."

"You watch too many cop shows," he said.

I poured us tumblers full of tequila with a squeeze of lime and showed him the money: $5,000. Gunther carried so much cash because it made him feel more like a man. Some man.

We sacked out the rest of the day. In the morning Billy left to take care of business, and I picked up the Caddy, paying Jeb in full. On my way back I saw an unmarked cruiser in front of the Blue Martini, which was closed until further notice. Tanya swept outside and watered cacti while inside a couple of detectives moseyed about.

"What's going on?" I asked her.

She looked over her shoulder, gave a nod, and pointed toward the subdivision.

"They questioned people who live over there. A few heard the shots, and now these cops are back here sniffing around. Who knows when I can open."

"I thought the police don't want to waste their energy on loser speed freaks."

"Apparently not every officer shares that sentiment."

Tanya must have noticed my concern, because she stopped watering and peered at me. "You doing okay? Must've been awful."

"I'm fine," I said, though I didn't sound fine. I wasn't fine.

"Hang tight. This'll all be over soon."

"Right." I headed back to my room, where I threw back a shot or two of tequila and fretted over what would come next.

When Billy showed up with takeout—guacamole, enchiladas, and chips from the Blue Coyote Restaurant out on Palm Canyon—he took one look at me and said, "What now?"

We ate in the room so we could talk privately, the swamp cooler working overtime.

I told him about the neighbors hearing shots.

Then I said, "What if someone says they heard the shots far apart?"

Billy sighed.

"Maybe it's time to leave," I said.

Billy stopped mid-bite. "You're going to Orange County?"

I shook my head and swabbed a chip in the guac. "I'm not going anywhere without you. Let's go to Mexico. While we can."

"I have my business, darlin'."

"You won't have it if you get thrown in jail. We could go down there and do something good, help women to leave bad men. Open a shelter."

"It's going to be fine."

"Ever the optimist," I said. I poured more hot sauce on my enchilada. Maybe it would burn away the worry festering.

In the morning, I woke up to a voicemail from that detective named Glen saying if it wasn't too much trouble, could I come in. They had a few more questions.

I stroked Billy's cheek to wake him and told him about the call.

"What'll I do?" I asked.

He pulled me to him, his body warm against mine. "Just go in and be your charming self," he said. Then he kissed me all over. I soon forgot my worries and succumbed. I had never had a more generous lover. Those women who think young dudes are better should wake up and smell the coffee.

Afterward I said, "I'm afraid."

He rubbed my back. "Shh," he said. "Go in and play dumb. If they try to get you to say why the shots were far apart, say the night was a jumble. There wasn't an insurance policy, right? Nothing you want from the asshole's estate?"

"What estate?" I said, calming down.

"There's no motive. What're they going to do? Nothing. They'll lose interest. I'm telling you, I know how these cops work."

"What if it doesn't go that way? What if they arrest me?"

"That ain't gonna happen."

I wasn't so sure, but I nodded. I showered while he went off to take care of rich people's yards. I put on my nicest sundress that showed my meager cleavage and rubbed honeysuckle oil behind my ears and across my wrists.

On my way to the cop shop, the Caddy hummed along, the hula girl on the dashboard shimmying to the vibration from the engine.

Glen, the detective who hated meth dealers, and the other one, who didn't so much care, led me into an interrogation room the size of a confessional that was all tans and whites. Glen offered me a soda or coffee. I said water would be fine.

They did what Billy thought. Asked me about the shots and the timing of the shots fired. I played dumb. That night I was so frazzled, so freaked out, I explained, and bunched my arms tighter to my body so they'd notice my boobs more than my replies.

And it sort of worked. With Glen, anyway. Though I still had a bad feeling, especially as Glen alone walked me to the door and thanked me for coming in. He suggested I get some therapy, that this had been a trauma that would likely haunt me for a long time.

I almost said, *Not more than Gunther alive haunted me.* He said they had all they needed, and it looked like they could close the case. But behind him, the other cop lingered and looked troubled as he watched me go.

Glen accompanied me all the way to the Caddy. I was glad to be away from the other cop. The sun swiped a silver brush stroke on the topside of Glen's hair. He gave me his card. On it he'd written his cell phone number.

"In case you think of something, or need to reach me," he said. "Or if you want to have a drink sometime."

I smiled, tried to keep the charm revved up. I told him I appreciated his softer dealings with me.

But as I accelerated down the road that could take me back to the Blue Martini, I knew my days in Palm Springs were numbered. It would be a matter of time before the other cop figured it out and came after me.

I also knew Billy hadn't been lying when he said he had a business he couldn't leave. And what he meant when he insisted I keep all of the money for myself.

I'd be far away from him if I kept driving south to Mexico. But I'd also be alone in Mexico rather than being confined to a jail cell. I squeezed the red steering wheel, sat up a little straighter, then took a quick moment to adjust my rearview mirror. My other mirrors were fine. I pressed on.

MAKING PEANUTS AT PACHANGA

Anna stood by the window of the fourteenth-floor hotel room her boyfriend, Rudy, booked for them. The beige earth of the desert stretched to the San Jacinto Mountains in the west. She flexed her bare feet, chewed a cuticle, and twirled her long red hair.

"Why'n't you get us a room at the Ritz-Carlton?" She rubbed at the smudge on the glass with the sleeve of her pullover and squinted in case that helped to see the Palm Springs tram edging its way up the mountain, but it was too bright out and the tram was too far away.

"No gambling there," he said. "Only tribal land in California allowed casinos."

"I'm not complaining. This is nice."

"I'm gonna look for ice." Rudy rolled off the bed, grabbed the bucket, and blew her a kiss at the door.

Rudy was a good guy, made money in construction and even wanted to help get her boy back from Jeremy, her soon-to-be ex-husband, who had custody of Tommy for the last year since he turned six. But he wanted to keep Tommy forever. Her son! You can kiss my ass, she told her ex. She spoke her mind and screw him if he didn't like it. Her parole officer said if she was to make progress in life, she needed to work on her attitude. *Where to begin.*

She tore open a packet of mixed nuts that lay on the table by the warm beers, cigarettes, and room key. Last meal she had was at Hadley's on the way here. Burger, fries, date shake. Her parents stopped at Hadley's when she was a little girl, when they were still a family, and she ordered a date shake back then, too, and slurped the cup dry.

On her phone's country playlist, Garth Brooks sang "Friends in Low Places."

"Damn straight," said Rudy, returning with the ice. "Only kinds of friends to have."

"Seriously?" she said. "I aspire to more than having loser friends."

Her comment rolled off him like water off a tarp. That's why they still got along. He never took her bad moods personally, and lately she was always in a bad mood. The longer she went without her boy, the worse she felt. Volunteering at the soup kitchen made her feel better, but she didn't know whether it was seeing people worse off than her or helping people that lifted her spirits. Regardless of the reason, she made a mental note to spend more time there.

Her sister told her she said novenas with her in mind, as if Saint what's-his-name, Judas, Jude, saint of lost causes, could help. She hated being thought of as a lost cause. She didn't pray to saints like her sister and mother did. If you prayed to saint whoever and got what you prayed for, wouldn't you forever be beholden to them? She didn't want to get stuck owing anything to anyone, especially a saint.

Rudy poured ice into the bathroom sink and, knowing him, he was in there arranging the bottles as if they were a work of art.

Salt from the peanuts stung her cut lip, already raw from gnawing it. "Those beers ready yet, Rude?"

"Babe. I just put them on ice." By the tone of his voice, she was trying his patience.

She popped a few more nuts into her mouth.

"You need to chill," he said, coming back into the room. "You got to be calm and collected when you see your PO. You're not going to get Tommy back if you throw one of your fits."

Anna wiped the sweat off her forehead as she padded across the carpet and turned the thermostat down to sixty-five degrees. The fan buzzed on. "Don't worry," she said, "I'll be calm and collected, like those people on TV ads for depression meds."

But she did worry because words leaked from her mouth as if they had a mind of their own. Bad luck with genetics. Her mother believed if she talked to God and prayed the rosary like a good Catholic, her problems would evaporate. Anna had tried it. She'd prayed and prayed but nothing happened. Other people with bigger problems taking up God's time? Without any help from Him, she gave up coke, her drug of choice, the one that got her arrested and made them take away her son. She was irritable most of the time, now, and even more unhappy than before, because not only did she not have Tommy, she was gaining weight. Her mother harangued her about her weight.

"A girl's got to stay thin for her man," her mother said, as if that should be Anna's goal in life: be thin, get a man, hooray!

Rudy lay back on the bed, pulling at his moustache as he flipped through the channels. "Hey, babe, you want that sapphire necklace? Look prettier on you than the chick on the screen. Pick up the phone."

"And you're going to pay for it, how?" asked Anna. "What I want is my boy. A boy belongs with his mother." The phone rang. Her arm jolted out to pick it up, and she almost knocked over the lamp.

"Calamity Jane," he said. "Take it easy."

Anna scowled as she held the phone to her ear and garbled words into it: yes, yes, she would.

She laid down the phone. "My PO is in the lobby." She looked into the mirror, slapped color into her sallow cheeks, and headed for the door.

"I'll come with you." Rudy pushed himself up off the bed.

"I can handle it."

"Okay, then." He fixed his eyes, the color of tree bark, on her and leaned onto the headboard nailed to the wall.

She padded down the dark hallway with the moss-green carpet designed by someone who must have been on acid—swirly paisley shapes, dots, and bubbles—and green-striped wallpaper. It was enough to give anyone a bad trip. She remembered the house she lived in when her parents were still together, before her cliché of a father ran off with his clichéd secretary. The patterned hallway offered no relief. It made her feel the walls were closing in.

She waited for the elevator. The day she met Jeremy, the hard Southern California winter rain fell as they stood beneath a towering palm tree whose fronds kept them dry. He was ten years older, almost thirty, and she was sure she would love him forever. A baby would make everything perfect, would get her out of the visually cluttered house she grew up in.

Jeremy didn't know she stopped using birth control. His own fault, thinking he didn't have to do anything, that it was up to her to make sure she didn't get pregnant. With a prissy name like Jeremy, she should have known what the future held.

She pressed the elevator button again. Her boy, Tommy, liked riding the elevator. He'd jump as it descended, boasting he could defy gravity, and it made her laugh. He was smart, her boy. Her mother claimed boys inherited smarts from their mothers. At least she had something going for her.

Nothing ever lasted, and who did Jeremy think he was, telling her they needed counseling because they argued. Everyone argued. She wasn't crazy. She didn't need a shrink. Jeremy was too damn serious. If she didn't give up coke, he said he'd leave her and take the boy. But the coke had kept her thin and interesting, and he liked her that way. A person couldn't win.

So much for vows of better or worse.

The doors opened and a stinking drunk stumbled out, held up by a brunette wearing a fur coat that engulfed everything but her head. As the door closed, the sorry dude fell on his face.

At the next floor a tall, muscular woman smelling of French fries and wearing a pink sequined gown stepped on. "Howdy, darlin'." She sounded more like a he.

Everybody wanted to be someone else. Anna wanted to be a good mother, free of cocaine, happy on her own. Good luck with that.

The elevator stopped again and three hammered blondes in dresses the size of G-strings stepped on.

One of the blondes frowned at Anna's unpedicured feet, another shot Anna a pitying smile. The third ignored her and said, "This guy I like, he's the sweetest thing, and rich."

Rich. Wouldn't that be nice. Imagine. The door opened onto the lobby. Why'd Rudy have to choose this place? It was the kind of hotel her ex would despise.

She passed parents with yowling brats and felt a pang of homesickness for Tommy. She'd take a whining kid over an absent one any day.

She stepped into the dining room lounge. There he sat, Mr. Upright Uptight Probation Officer. White shirt, striped tie, short brown grammar school haircut. He sat at a square table, back straight, hands clasped in front of him.

He held the keys to her damn future. She could use a Camel about now, filterless, strong. "Mr. LeTay," she said. The dude had as much facial expression as a crow.

"Anna, how are you?"

"I'm okay, and you?"

He stood as she sat.

"Look," he said. "I'll cut right to the chase. The court doesn't look kindly on the possession of cocaine or violating probation. And remember, you left town."

"I ran out of money," she said. "I had to get a job."

A waitress with pointy boobs out to here and a skirt up to there, said, "Care for something, hon?"

"Bloody Mary."

LeTay gave her a puzzled expression, as if she was an animal he'd never seen.

That's right—on probation she wasn't supposed to drink. "Sorry—I meant tomato juice."

He ordered club soda with lime. The waitress scurried away. LeTay hated her, despised her, and she couldn't care less. Maybe she cared a little.

"The way the court sees it, you abandoned your son," he said. "Did you?"

"Did I what? Abandon Tommy? Of course not!"

"Why did you leave, then?"

"I was making peanuts at Pechanga," she said. "Casinos in Vegas pay better. Tommy's father said he'd care for him while I was gone. Only six months! But I'm back now. I'm back."

LeTay rattled on about how Tommy was a good kid, but he lacked feeling. "He displays antisocial behavior. He has a problem showing empathy for others and letting himself feel emotions."

"Feeling too much isn't good." Anna licked the tomato juice from the celery. "When he was a little boy, and I'm talking little, this balloon man came up to Tommy at the fair, wanted to make him a balloon creature, a dog, a kitty. Tommy accepted a sword. He just wasn't like other little kids. He knows things no kid his age knows. My son is very intelligent. When he was four, he could beat all of us at poker."

LeTay made her squirm. It was as if he could see straight into her brain and read her thoughts. She stopped talking.

"The boy's very unhappy. He feels you deserted him."

She downed the rest of her drink. "Who do you think I am, to do a thing like that?" she said. Her tongue wagged, and her mouth moved independent of her brain. She sounded like her dad when she told him she was pregnant with Tommy and was leaving home. Her dad's angry red face while her mom kept crossing herself, moving her mouth to a silent prayer.

LeTay's eyes gave him away. The more she ranted, the further away he moved from that place of helpfulness.

Across the room a clamoring slot machine crapped quarters into a little old lady's paper cup. Anna had never been any good at gambling. When she was little, her dad kept a one-armed bandit covered with a canvas tarp in the basement under the pool table. After school she slid it out and her friends fed it pennies, shrieking when three of the same fruit lined up. Anna liked lemons the best. Just saying the word "lemon" set her mouth to watering.

"What are your plans?" LeTay's voice drew her back to the room.

"Plans?"

"Have an attorney?" He took an ice cube into his mouth and slogged it around.

"Do I need one?"

His forehead and eyes scrunched together, like her dad's. His eyes were topaz like her dad's too, bordering on yellow.

"You haven't been in touch with Tommy's father, I take it."

"You from the South?" she said.

"Long time ago," he said.

"Name like LeTay, I figured. My dad's from Louisiana. You sound like him."

He looked at his expensive watch. He wasn't going to let her schmooze him.

"There will be another hearing. In the meantime, Tommy will remain with his father."

Another slot machine screeched. Anna had to get out of there, get to Tommy before Jeremy turned him against her. Her head hurt. The ceiling in the lounge was too damn low; the floors above pressed down on her.

"You can visit your son," he said. "He's at the social services administration. I'll drive you."

She felt her face flush the way it did when she was about to go off. Her ex didn't know who he was messing with. Just let him try to keep her son.

They walked from the casino into the desert heat that boiled her bones. The car was even hotter.

"Mind turning up the air-conditioning?" she asked as LeTay cruised away from the hotel.

The fan blew back her hair as they drove. He pulled into a parking lot and into a space before a dirt-colored prefab building.

The car hadn't even come to a stop when she was out the door and inside the building so fast the woman behind the counter spun around and held her heart. "Ooo, you gave me a fright! Can I help you?"

Anna tried catching her breath. "My son, Tommy Hunter. I came to see him."

"Let me see." The woman looked at a file. LeTay stepped up to the counter. When the woman saw him, her voice turned singsong-y. "Hi there, Albert. How you been?"

"Never better. You're looking good, Donna."

"Always the charmer," Donna said.

Anna was about to lose it, goo-goo eyes going on around her. Donna held out something to Anna. A slippery cool beaded thing fell into her open palm.

"Tommy must've dropped it last time he was here," said Donna. "Want to give it to him? People's rosaries are such special things. Mother Mary is an example for us all."

A phone rang and Donna picked it up. LeTay paced, jingling change in his pants pockets. Anna believed in omens, but what sort of omen was this, Donna handing her a rosary that belonged to her son? When the hell had Jeremy gone the Catholic way? Now he was filling Tommy's head with propaganda.

Her lungs contracted. The light dimmed. She had busted her butt for Jeremy. Her love of illegal substances had nothing to do with him or her son. All the moms at Tommy's school took pills, or they snorted or drank one thing or another. She was the one who got caught.

The rosary with its brown wooden beads lay in her palm. She imagined Jeremy getting down on his knees, saying the rosary with Tommy, droning those not entirely unpleasant words. A ray of sun streamed through the window and blasted her hand with light. The little metal face of Mary that held the string together lit up like a flame and she gasped. It was as if Mary was looking straight into her eyes, telling her she just had to try a little harder, her son was still within reach, that the songs of the saints would reach her ears, if only she would listen.

Show me how to listen, she thought. *Show me.*

Down the hallway a door opened. Tommy. He shuffled toward her. She was so far from the person she wanted to be, the girl she once was. She knew of others, redeemed from fates worse than hers. The crucifix from the rosary bit into her palm. When she opened her fist, a drop of blood hit the floor.

PINK AVIARY

Twin Peaks, the three-legged, orange radio-and-TV tower atop the highest hill in San Francisco, looms over my neighborhood. When the Big One hits, it's a straight shot from the tower to the Mars Street house where I live, and with my luck, the tower will skewer us like a shish kebab. Cantilevered houses cling to the sides of hills like barnacles, not unlike me clinging to life in this city. Streets adjacent to Mars are named after the planets. There's no end to the jokes about the street named Uranus. San Francisco has the best sense of humor of anywhere I've ever lived.

Lately, though, I haven't felt much like laughing. It's hard being broke anywhere, but it's especially difficult here, where a cappuccino can set you back six bucks. My job as a server at the Yellow Rose doesn't bring in nearly enough.

I moved here a year ago from Orange County, four hundred miles to the south. I was a broken woman but not without hope when I auditioned for top-tier and mid-tier dance companies, as well as dance ensembles around the state. Then I lost my job teaching at a dance school because the owner's daughter decided she wanted to teach, and I was let go. I tried to get my cousin Mimi, born the same day and year as me, to move north, but she loves Orange County and wants to snag a rich dude.

So I moved and burrowed in, hoping a dance company would have me, or a dance studio. I cross my fingers that my dream of dreams happens, that the dance company I auditioned for last week will want me. Any minute I should hear.

I met my best friend, Tammy, also a server, at the Yellow Rose, a Tex-Mex restaurant over the hill in the Haight. The owners threw a party at their Marin County ranch. I drank three vodka martinis and played an adult version of Truth or Dare where I stripped down to my birthday suit and did jumping jacks. That made Tammy think I was wilder than I am and want to know me better.

Tammy left the Yellow Rose when she applied to graduate school for psychology, because grad school costs money and she needed more, so she got a job working as an exotic dancer at the Pink Aviary in the Tenderloin, a low-rent district that's home to the most high school dropouts in the city. Tammy is tiny, with big hips, and dances with wild abandon. Her boyfriend knows she sees other guys, but he's smitten and overlooks what he calls her passionate indiscretions. She loves the job but hates the men's—and sometimes women's—fingers roaming as they stuff twenties under her G-string. I'd hate that, too, though the cash would be nice.

Tammy and I meet for coffee near the Pink Aviary. We sit by the big glass window and brainstorm what I could do for money. She brings up dancing again.

"The tech district dudes adore the Aviary." Tammy pats her purple glossed lips with a napkin. "They think no one will see them, but everyone ends up there."

"The wrong head is doing the thinking," I say. "But I can't do what you do."

"You can! You tear up the dance floor, and with your body, you'd get so many tips. If I can with my raisin boobs, think of what you'd get with your watermelons."

"They're not watermelons," I say.

"Cantaloupes, then."

"Maybe pears."

"Pears. Melons. Whatever."

A few nights a week Tammy and I go to clubs in North Beach or south of Market. Sometimes we go so crazy on the dance floor that people move out of our way to watch.

"If this dance company comes through," I say, "I can get my grandmother's ring back."

"It's that bad? Do you need to borrow some money?"

"I sold my car, but thanks. My cousin Mimi said if I go back to OC, I can stay with her, but if I have to listen to how smart and pretty Ann Coulter is, my head will explode."

"Who talks about Ann Coulter anymore?"

"Orange County Republicans, that's who. She's their goddess."

Tammy holds up her petite hands. "I get it. You could always marry that rich guy you told me about, the one who leaves you twenty-dollar tips."

"He's too into himself. He gets manicures."

"That's not right," she says. "Meet me tomorrow night at the club. I'll introduce you to the manager."

"I'm not going to be an exotic dancer," I say.

"You deserve to make good money dancing."

"It's just not me," I say.

"Then just meet me for a drink."

I give in, say I will, and she excuses herself to use the restroom. While she's gone, I check the email on my phone to see if there's anything from the dance company. Nothing yet.

The next night I take a trolley down Market back to the Tenderloin, checking my cell phone way too much. I mosey a few blocks over to the Pink Aviary.

The plain redbrick exterior belies what's inside. Ropes of pink twinkle lights hang along pink brocade walls and crisscross the ceiling. Little round tables with pink tablecloths under round sheets of glass and, on top, pink carnations in white hobnail vases give the place a tea shop vibe. The room smells like incense and alcohol. On either side of the stage, women dance on pedestals inside white metal birdcages. Acid pink velveteen curtains back the stage, and in its center a woman wearing a skirt made of feathers swirls about trancelike to "(I Can't Get No) Satisfaction." She's got to be on something: Oxy, Vicodin, booze. Maybe that's what it takes to dance in a place like this.

Tammy's neither at the bar nor at a table, and I turn to go, when a woman in the teensiest pink sequined bikini top and pink sequined chaps that show her toned heinie says, "Don't be shy. Go on in and take a seat."

"I'm meeting a friend," I say.

"Your friend'll find you."

The only other woman in the audience is a skinny redhead wearing a shiny emerald-green halter and hat. She sits among a group of men. So many men—in suits, in flannel shirts, alone, and in groups—who all look a little glazed. Neckties are loose, top buttons undone.

I take a small round table covered with a pink tablecloth. I sniff the flowers. No smell whatsoever. Fake flowers, made of silk.

I like men, not women, but the dancers *are* titillating, all that shimmying and thrusting their rear ends at the audience, all that sliding up and down the poles in their cages.

A man in a black pinstripe suit stops at my table and says, "Is this chair taken?" The pink-sequined hottie sets a sloe gin fizz, the specialty of the house, on the table before me.

"It *will* be when my friend arrives." The pink drink makes me happy for a moment.

"I'll warm it up for him."

"Her," I say, draining the glass. Must be all ice.

"I'm Rob." He sits down with his highball.

"Nice anonymous name."

"And you are?"

"Waiting."

"That's an unusual name." He scoots his chair closer to mine. "You don't often see women here alone."

"First time for everything. I told you, I'm waiting for a friend." And for an email or financial help so I can get Granny's ring back and not lose my apartment.

I tip back my glass and catch an ice shard with my tongue.

On stage a dancer does an elaborate shimmy with a swath of peacock feathers. It's bizarre but entrancing, the way she moves to the soundtrack of ambient jungle noises and a backbeat of drums.

He appraises me. "You should dance here. You have the body for it. You'd be good."

"You've known me all of two minutes."

"I'm a good judge of people."

"I get cold easy."

"You can use a boa. Feathers keep birds warm."

"House of the Rising Sun" comes on. The lights on stage dim, then come up bright pink. Rob finishes off his drink. Another server in pasties and chaps with a butt as smooth and round as a honeydew appears.

He points his thumb at me. "Another highball, and whatever she's drinking."

Honeydew leaves with our order. He has dark hair that brushes his collar and a nine o'clock shadow that's probably on purpose, and he has a cleft in his chin that looks like a baby's butt.

He reminds me of an actor from the old foreign films I used to be addicted to.

Rob leans over and runs his finger along my collarbone.

"My favorite part of a woman's body," he says.

"Mine too." I toss his hand away.

I check my phone—to see if there's a message from Tammy and to see if there's anything from the dance company. Nothing from either one.

Another round of drinks arrives. The room fills up. Few tables are free. More women than I expected, with men and by themselves. I check my email and there's one from the dance company. I'm about to open it, when Tammy whispers in my ear.

"Darling," she says, and pulls up a chair on the other side of me. She calls me "darling" in public; she likes men to think we're gay. "Who's your friend?" She tweaks her chin toward Rob.

I introduce them and Tammy's face lights up.

"Wait," she says, "I know you."

At the same time, he says, "I've seen your act."

"Big tipper." Tammy winks and elbows me.

"I heard from them." I'm hardly able to contain my glee over the email.

"What'd they say?" She's excited right along with me. "Read it!"

I open the email as a server Tammy knows brings her a pink martini, and she holds it up, ready to toast my good news.

But it's not good news.

I put down my phone, feeling more dejected than I've ever felt.

"It's okay." I raise my glass. Tammy and Rob raise their glasses, and we toast.

"To better times," Tammy says, and I drink. She hesitates before she sips from her drink. "What'd they say?"

"They wished me luck."

"Fuck them," she says.

"I told her she should dance here," Rob says.

"Yes!" says Tammy.

An older man with a beer belly and a shirt open to his navel and chest hair blooming from the top approaches the table.

"They're still talking about your act last night," he says to Tammy. His Brooklyn accent is as thick as an egg cream.

"You were great," says Rob.

Tammy flashes a toothy smile and introduces me to the manager, Ian.

Ian says, "You dance?"

"You should see her," says Tammy. "She was a dancer in New York."

"Philadelphia," I say.

"One of my girls called in sick tonight," Ian says. "Show us what you got."

"Do it!" Tammy claps her hands double-time.

"I'm n-not prepared," I stammer. The room is spinning from the sloe gin fizzes I guzzled. I'm such a lightweight when it comes to alcohol.

"What's to prepare?" says Ian. "If you're a dancer, you dance."

Tammy leans over and whispers, "Just pretend you're dancing with me."

Ian presses his hand into my shoulder, and it's as if he just hit a lever that releases me from my seat, because I follow him to the dressing room.

"Stay loose," he says. "Give it your best, pick a song you know."

"How about 'Girls, Girls, Girls'?" I say.

"Good choice."

Ian leaves me with a selection of feather boas in various shades of pink and a new G-string—at least I hope it's new. My stomach churns with nerves and sweat is pouring down my face, which I wipe with a towel. Fluff out my hair. Do some deep breathing.

Ten minutes later I'm wrapped in a flamingo-pink boa and onstage behind the closed curtain. Two girls wearing feather pasties over their nipples stand in the cages, making adjustments to their boas. One looks me over and winks.

The first chord of "Girls, Girls, Girls" is my cue. The curtains part. Under the pink lights, the audience is sheathed in black.

Pretend no one's there. Pretend you're ten years old again and in the basement dancing to "Daydream Believer."

Before long the G-string is all I'm wearing. I shimmy and gyrate and dance like nobody's watching. I burn with the music.

Tammy and Rob call out, "You go, girl." Whistles and hoots fire me up even more. I do things with the pole I didn't even know were possible. The room is a blur. The audience is with me. Men will think of me when they're back in their beds or bathrooms. I've had this happen before dancing, reaching a trance state when you forget about the audience, and your body and the music become one. There's nothing better.

As the song winds down, I finish lying on my side, my head propped up with my hand. The audience goes wild. I'm crying tears of joy or relief, because this was good, a reward of sorts. Maybe I *could* do this. Maybe it's not such a bad thing.

The curtains close. The audience continues to howl in drunken appreciation.

"You're good," Ian says when he comes onto the stage.

I wipe my eyes with the back of my hand. He helps me up as the cage dancers climb down off their perches. "You got the job if you want it," he says. "You got me all worked up, sweetheart, and it takes a lot to get Ian worked up." He pronounces worked "woiked" and gives a quick matter-of-fact squeeze to the lump in his pants.

Ian can't tear his eyes from my breasts, but I don't care.

"You in?" he says.

I say sure. I dress and hotfoot it out of there. I don't want to see Tammy just yet. She'll congratulate me for getting a job that pays ten times more than the Yellow Rose. On the one hand, it's blissful; on the other, it's depressing as hell.

The fog rolls in, and the mist on my face feels like a blessing. Maybe it won't be so bad. I grab a trolley to Grant Street in Chinatown, a festive one-way, one-lane street jammed with stores and restaurants on both sides. The street is lit up and clogged with tourists and fried food smells. Jade and pearls glimmer in shop windows. Headless mannequins wear satin robes. I covet a red floor-length silk kimono, mind-numbing in its beauty. Price tag says $199, but when you're broke, $200 is a fortune. Yet I won't be broke for long, thanks to my screwed-up luck.

My phone vibrates with a text from Tammy: "WTF?"

I text back and say to meet me at the He She Love Acts club down on Columbus, near Grant.

I go into the club, order a vodka tonic, and settle in to watch the show. The stage is darkly lit. A woman dances languidly—the warm-up act. If I'm going to be an exotic dancer, I should study, right?

Tammy texts to say Rob and she are on their way.

I text, "Great," but I don't know if it *is* great. Sometimes I can't tell where the line is. My mother, with her string of boyfriends while still married to my dad, taught me the boundaries are where you put them. But that can't be right. My own boundaries are as flexible as a rope of kelp.

Rob and Tammy arrive ten minutes later.

"You crazy, girl!" She riffles my hair but sees my sad face. "You'll get over the dance company thing," she says.

"Right," I say. "It's nothing."

"Liked your dance." Rob looks at me as if I'd cast a spell.

"Just a dance," I say.

The handsome guys always think you like them, but I'm not on the market. My next boyfriend isn't going to hang out at clubs gawking at naked women.

Onstage a guy and girl are getting it on. Tammy and Rob are fixated. So am I. Is it even legal to do this in public? Nudity is legal in SF; you can go around naked as long as you place a towel on public benches before you sit, but this is extreme.

When the curtain falls, Tammy says, "That was hot!"

Rob fans himself. "Let's get a room."

"You paying?" says Tammy.

"There's a boutique hotel just up the street."

"You down?" Tammy asks me.

I swallow the rest of my drink. Everything and everyone has a burnished glow. I'm not sure I can stand up.

"I should get home," I say. I lament the girl I once was who danced every Christmas in the *Nutcracker Suite*, who went to college, who once imagined herself an artist. Friends said if anyone could make it as a dancer, it was me.

"Ah, come on." Tammy slings her arm through mine.

"Yeah, come on." Rob pays for our drinks. He drops a ten on the table for a tip.

"We'll celebrate your new job." Tammy winks.

My legs carry me to a penthouse suite with thick burgundy drapes and two bedrooms. I mean to ask, "Why two?" when Rob says he's going next door to buy us a bottle of something good and to get comfy.

Tammy pulls open the closet. "Check out these robes, girlfriend."

Then Rob's back with a bottle of Dom Perignon, a bottle of vodka, and two bottles of tonic water. He finds four glasses on a shelf in a cabinet. I'm about to ask, "Why four?" when there's a knock.

"Ran into a buddy at the liquor store." Rob lets in a burly guy, beefy and handsome in an Aryan sort of way, if you like the type. Tammy has a million types. He studies us as if we are entrees he looks forward to tasting.

Rob introduces Nils and hands us glasses, then cues up Beyoncé on his iPhone. Tammy engages Nils in a dance. That leaves Rob and me. I lose track of how many glasses of Champagne I consume. Rob peels back my robe and lets it fall. Nils and Tammy go into the other bedroom.

Rob steps out of his pants. He pulls me to him.

"You need to use a condom," I say.

"Okay," he says, "Whatever you want." He's a good kisser, but somewhere in my brain I wonder what the hell I'm doing in this room with a stranger, while my best—and only—friend in this city is in the other room with a man who looks like a character from the movie *Blade Runner.*

Rob tries to push into me.

"Where's the condom?" I say.

"Ah, come on, don't be like that," he says.

"No, really, you need one." I'm slurring more than a little.

"Just this once," he says.

He won't let up and makes me mad, so I give him a little push, but I push too hard because he falls off me, hits his head on the nightstand, and is out cold.

I kneel before Rob and hold my finger to his nose to see if he's breathing. He is, but he won't wake up.

"Tammy," I call.

In between moans, she says, "What?"

"I could use your help in here!"

Tammy sees me on the floor beside the bed. This gets her attention. "What happened?"

She bends over Rob.

Nils lifts him onto the bed and tries to revive him. I pull on my clothes and call 9-1-1.

"What are you doing?" Tammy says.

"He needs a hospital."

There's nothing like an accident to sober you up real fast. Tammy, Nils, and I wait in the lobby of the ER. Nils pages through a *People* magazine. Tammy gets up in my face, says, "Why'd you push him? We were all having such a great time."

"*You* were having a great time," I say. "I was only there because *you* wanted to be there."

"You really should loosen up, Gemma. That's your problem. That's probably why you can't get a dancing gig. You're so uptight."

That's when I see Tammy for who she is.

"Rob's your friend." I gather my things. "This happened because of you. I'm out of here."

"You can't leave," she says.

But I'm out of there in less time than it takes to say, "Oh, yes, I can."

I catch a bus to Market Street, then another bus to my flat on Mars. I phone Mimi and ask her if the offer still holds.

"Come on down," she says, reminding me of Bob Barker on the old *The Price Is Right*. "I found my prince. Maybe he has a friend for you."

"Please, no more men for now," I say. "I'm happy to see you, though."

I throw my things into suitcases, take my savings out from under the mattress, all $112 dollars of it, and call an Uber.

If I don't leave the city now, I never will. This place is like a boyfriend you obsess over because he never wants you as much as you want him. You keep trying because you're sure things will change, but they never do.

I clean up, empty the trash, and leave a message at the pawn shop about the ring, saying I'll send money in a week or so. I drop the key in the mailbox and a message on the property manager's voicemail saying to keep my deposit for my last month's rent.

An Uber delivers me and my life contained in two suitcases to the bus station. As we speed down Market Street, the storefronts, cafes, and clubs blur by. The fog lifts. The sky is clear, bright with the full moon. I will miss the Lotus Garden restaurant in Chinatown. I will miss Golden Gate Park's Conservatory of Flowers. I will miss how the fogbank rolls in and engulfs Twin Peaks.

My phone vibrates with a text from Tammy, saying Rob's going to be okay, that he just has a concussion. I don't text back.

At the bus station, I stash my luggage in the compartment beneath the seats and mount the steps to the bus that will deliver me to the great red county to the south. We pull away from the station and head for the Bay Bridge. As we leave the city of hard-luck tales, I begin to relax. A woman beside me pulls a Baggie of frozen grapes from a travel-size cooler. She holds out the bag to me.

"You ever taste 'em this way?" she says. "They're good."

I thank her and bite into the frozen pulp. At first the cold hurts my teeth, then it's refreshing. The woman offers another. I savor it as the bus motors onto the lower deck of the Bay Bridge. A pair of gulls lift into the sky, the neon from a nearby bar turning their white feathers pink.

ANIMALS

A twilight sky like faded lilacs. Earth damp from mist. Evening air scented jasmine. On the outskirts of Los Angeles, it was typical fall weather. Our vans swept into the parking lot. Langdon, in a mask and hoodie, awaited us. He'd gone ahead on his Harley to scout and make sure everything was good.

Headlights off, doors open. Ivy and I and a handful of volunteers donned white masks, pulled up our hoodies, and jumped from the vans. I followed behind Ivy, who was as strong and graceful as a Bengal tiger.

My temples pulsed as we rushed to the lab's entrance. Usually, these protests exhilarated me. What we did was vital work, saving animals from the lab hacks who performed meaningless tests on them, all in the name of creating safe makeup for women, but this raid had me chewing my lips raw.

Ivy, founder of SAFE (Saving Animals from Evil), pulled at the heavy green metal doors. They wouldn't budge. My heart wrestled with itself as I used a lock pick earring I bought at a crafts fair and jiggled it in the deadbolt. Langdon, tall and rangy as a panther, with a beard and hair as black, came up behind us and said, "I'll kick down the fucking door."

"A metal reinforced door?" Ivy looked as stressed as I'd ever seen her. "Good luck."

Langdon was full of himself, as always. Part of his charm.

The lock gave, and the three of us advanced into the lobby while the remaining volunteers waited outside the doors and with the vans, prepared to deliver the animals to safe houses and sanctuaries.

We slid past the guard's metal desk littered with fast food wrappers and empty Big Gulp cups. I'd monitored the lab for weeks, and unless schedules changed, right now the guard strolled the exterior of this building and any structures connected to it, checking doors and windows and whatever else guards did.

Last night I'd timed him: twenty-two minutes.

"Something feels off," I said as our shoes squeaked across the polished cement floor.

"Be specific," Ivy said.

I jogged to keep up with her. "It's like when the weatherman says it's going to be a clear day, but you smell ozone in the air and know it's going to storm. Like that."

Ivy shook her head. "Try to focus, Giselle. *Focus.*" Ivy had been involved in major raids, but I had never done anything like this. I'd been on protests—picketed pet stores that imported tropical fish, furriers, circuses—but I hadn't been involved in anything that could get me arrested.

We pushed through a second set of doors into a room with animals in cages and buzzing fluorescent lights.

"Jesus," Ivy said.

Two dozen howling, barking, and baying dogs—beagles because their sweet, submissive natures made them a preferred breed for cosmetic testing. Cats' ears flattened like kites; they sounded an eerie human-baby cry. Long-eared bunnies squealed.

I had never been inside a lab like this. The smell stung my nose. Ammonia, urine, BO. What would drive a person to work here? Who would allow themselves to be trained and hardened into seeing animals as objects with the sole purpose of serving humans and tortured so women could buy waterproof mascara?

Ivy's words from our meetings hammered my brain: *"We will be the Rosa Parks of the animal activist movement."*

That possibility made the risk worth it.

Langdon sauntered down the hallway to the back of the lab while Ivy and I opened cages. I had practiced for hours picking locks open, releasing hundreds of combinations in preparation for tonight. Ivy commended me for my nimble fingers, said I should have been a surgeon (but I hate the site of blood so never mind), and I absorbed her praise like the desert absorbs rain. SAFE was lucky to have me, she said, and made me feel indispensable. Everyone wants to be one of a kind, missed when they're gone.

I knelt before the first cage. The lock refused to open.

"Please," I whispered.

Finally, thankfully, the lock released. One after another, ecstatic dogs leapt to their freedom, toenails clicking as they slipped and slid across the cement floor toward the exit.

One skinny, floppy-eared pup refused to leave the cage. The more I said, "It's okay, buddy," the louder he howled. I said I'd be back and took care of the remaining creatures.

Ten minutes later most of the vans had left with dogs, leaving two vans—one for the cats and bunnies and remaining volunteers and one for Ivy and me. We released the cats into cardboard carriers that volunteers ferried to another van. Instead of putting the bunnies in crates, I ran them out to the grassy mound under a stand of conifers and let them go. They froze, as if they didn't know what to do with their freedom in the wild.

"Go." I waved my hands. "*Go!*"

I ran inside to the cage of the stubborn puppy. He pressed into the corner, growling. I didn't want to get bitten, but we were out of time. I offered him a treat, said, "Sh, sh," grabbed him by the scruff, and ran him out to a van about to pull away.

With the animals gone, the room grew as quiet as a cave. If only the animals in labs could talk, the stories they could tell.

But where was Langdon? My gut screamed. In five minutes, the guard would be back. My brain was about to short circuit, when he emerged from the dark back hallway. Ivy was irritated with him in a way foreign to me. They'd always gotten along well.

At the guard's desk, Langdon said, "You two ought to get going. I'll catch up with you later."

"No rats, mice, or guinea pigs here," I said as we moved across the lot to the van, the gravel hard under my feet. "Strange."

"This lab prefers pets," said Ivy. "Which means they're using bunchers and dealers."

At meetings, Ivy told us bunchers were people who kidnapped pets or responded to free pet ads only to turn around and sell the animals to dealers, who in turn sold them to labs.

"The dealers are who you really want," Ivy said, strapping in. "But they're dangerous."

Once the van rounded a curve, she pulled over, and we jumped out to remove the license plate covers. Back in the van, Ivy felt around in the console for her cigarettes.

"Let me help you." I lit a filterless Pall Mall for her and said, "That went great!" I was so excited we had pulled it off. Headlights flashed against Ivy's face. Her jaw looked tight. She did the poker face better than anyone I knew.

"Fantastic," she said, but her voice sounded strained.

Inside Ivy's condo, "Where Is the Love" by the Black Eyed Peas played as volunteers drifted in and popped open beers.

Ivy fished a beer out of a cooler someone had donated, handed it to me, and tinked the bottle with her own.

"Aren't you excited?" I asked.

"I'm just tired," Ivy said. "You did good." She pasted on a smile.

We'd done something important and useful. "I feel great!"

Ivy nodded and gobbled a handful of chips.

Maybe the more events you were a part of, the rush grew old.

Twenty minutes later Langdon barged through the door.

Ivy frowned. "What took you so long?"

His response was a twisted, devilish grin. "We got them good."

"What are you saying?" she said.

"The lab. Who else?" He hiked his shoulders and merged into the group in the kitchen. He gave me this look as he slugged from the bottle. A chill ran down my spine. When I was a kid, my mother said chills were an omen. She'd say, "Somebody just walked over your future grave."

Ivy was watching him, worry lines creasing her usually smooth forehead.

"Why do you look so bummed?" I said. "We had a victory, right?"

"He worries me," she said.

In the living room, volunteers, mostly college students like me, passed joints as Justin Timberlake sang "Cry Me a River."

From across the room Langdon shot me a toothy smile, and I gave him a fake one back. I told Ivy I had to take off. I lived at home during the summer break and wanted to get on the road before it grew too late.

The entire way I sang to Sheryl Crow's *C'mon, C'mon* CD.

I tried not to worry. If something went wrong, breaking into a lab could garner us misdemeanors or worse, but what could go wrong? Unless we'd been caught in the act, no one would ever know who we were. Though the cameras had likely caught our actions, our hoodies and masks had obscured our faces. SAFE had no office that authorities could raid, no forms volunteers filled out, no way to track down its members. Of the two dozen people who attended meetings, only Ivy, Langdon, and I knew one another's last names. All perfectly anonymous.

The house was dark. At the front door my mother's dog, Poppy, a little white Bichon mix she adopted from the pound when I went to college, sniffed my feet. My mother went to bed by ten and said she slept like the dead. I didn't want to wake her.

In the bathroom I washed my hands, splashed water on my face. Poppy followed me up to my room. I dropped my clothes to the carpet and climbed into bed. Sleep refused to come. I was still wound up from doing good, saving animals, and making history.

When the curtains lit up with the morning sun, I straggled downstairs to the kitchen where Mom sipped her milky Folgers and worked the Jumble in the comics section. The kitchen was too bright, and I shaded my eyes with my fingers until my eyes grew used to the light.

She jumped up to give me a hug. "Giselle! You should have woken me up when you got in."

"You like your sleep." I took a mug down from the shelf.

She gestured with her chin at Mr. Coffee. "It's strong the way you like it."

I was still feeling elated when I saw the *Santa Barbara Press* lying on the counter. On the front page a photograph of a fire and a short article. I pulled the paper toward me, sipped the strong brew, and read:

". . . Authorities are investigating a fire that destroyed the Layne Laboratories. SAFE, an animal rights group that fights what they call 'speciesism' is suspected to be behind the raid. Eco-terrorist groups like SAFE also practice 'extensional self-defense' that argues since animals can't fight back themselves, human beings should act as proxies."

Terrorist? I'd only wanted to save the animals. I felt cold all over the way I did when I was about to faint.

My mother set down her cup. "You look pale," she said, and poured me a glass of pineapple juice. "Sip."

I hung my head between my legs. Poppy must have sensed my nervous system shorting out because he hopped around me, barking.

We burned down a building? We are so, so screwed. Langdon, the bastard.

"What's wrong?" Mom said. "Talk to me."

Images and sounds churned through my brain. The guard's desk with the Big Gulp. Animals' cries. The little dog that didn't want to leave. Langdon's glimmery eyes at Ivy's.

"I'll be right back," I said, and took the stairs two at a time. Poppy scooted behind. I dropped onto the mattress and the pooch jumped on and sat before me, alert. Tears soaked my face. Poppy licked my hand. I hugged the ball of fur so hard he whimpered.

My mother would freak out if she knew what I did the night before. I should have been in the darkroom printing photographs for next week's class. There was Spanish to study and history on the Native Americans who settled in the Central Coast. I should have been anywhere but where I was. I used to imagine my future like the midway at the county fair, lit up on all sides with possibilities, but now I was certain those lights had all but burned out.

NOISE

It was as if there were construction workers downstairs in Coco's living room. She threw off the covers and spun down the winding staircase. Her cat, Tiny Man, pawed at the front door. Poor thing—the sound affected him as much, if not more, than Coco. She yanked open the door to investigate, and Tiny Man sprang outside, running for his life.

The teeth-bending clamor that began every day at seven a.m. sharp came from next door. The quiet atmosphere that had originally attracted Coco to the prosaic Irvine condo complex, with its twisty-turny walkways and chemically treated, man-made babbling brooks, had become a cacophony of ear-splitting noise pollution.

At thirty-five, she had developed an allergy to noise. Noise followed Coco like a stray dog. Noise was why she left her Costa Mesa apartment complex. Here she sought relief from the salsa music, techno-pop, and sportos hollering in front of the TV. In this master-planned, supposedly sedate city of Irvine, a steady stream of laborers kept the decibel level in the red, thanks in large part to the gardeners and their best friend, the leaf blower.

Coco couldn't take it anymore. She threw a hot-pink terrycloth robe on over her black PJs with the roller skates motif, a birthday gift from her best friend, Mona; slipped into her orange flip-flops; and marched next door, but not before looking in the mirror and fluffing up her short pitch-black hair. Not a great look for a hair stylist.

Her next-door neighbor, Tom Fields-Jackson, leaned on the outer wall of his living room, bracing himself against the planter.

"What the hell's wrong with you?" she yelled through his metal gate.

When he saw her coming, he tensed up and mouthed, *Oh my God.* He wore headphones while a laborer tore apart his cement-slab patio. His eyelids fluttered as if blinking away a speck of sand.

When he didn't respond, Coco bounded through the gate and lifted one noise-canceling ear pad away from his head. "This sound is driving me crazy!"

Tom jerked away. The ear pad slapped his head. "I'm tired of you hassling me," he said. "Chill!"

He was an asshole—a *cute* asshole, with a five o'clock shadow, skin-tight jeans, and a T-shirt that clung to his body like a wetsuit. He wore green high-top Converse and had dyed black hair like hers. His tats transformed the skin of his arms into a fine patterned fabric. He had no flaws she knew of except for his name: Fields-Jackson. Hyphenated last names made her want to scream.

He was her type, dammit, which made his lack of neighborliness worse. Guys younger and hotter than he flirted with her, so why not him? Was it because she wasn't a blue-eyed blonde?

Tom and Coco faced off. He yanked his cell phone from his jeans and said, "Dude, you better go. I'm calling the cops."

The laborer, with a trimmed goatee and deep dimples, put down the jackhammer. The morning turned as quiet as a church. If only it was always like this.

Tom Fields-Jackson fluttered his tan fingers, silver bands halfway down his thumbs, instructing the laborer to ignore her and keep working.

"I will take a break." The laborer fetched his Thermos and disappeared through the gate.

"I mean it," Tom said to Coco. "I'm calling." He held up his cell phone.

"I'm not done with you, dude," she said as she clicked the gate closed behind her.

It was high school all over again: boys who ignored her, girls who teased because she was so tall, teachers who scowled when she knew more than them. She rushed home before she ended up doing something she'd be sorry for.

Coco showered to cool off, gelled her hair, and pulled at the tips to make them stand out like quills. For breakfast she made a lima bean–tofu scramble with rice-bread toast and chili-pepper marmalade. Her next-to-the-last ex said her food choices matched her personality. She took it as a compliment. They stayed together for two years—a record for her.

Her last boyfriend, in the beginning, called her his muse, but "muse" turned to "mess" and one morning he was gone. No note, no *farewell, it's been nice knowing you*. Just gone.

From her dining room window, she ate her breakfast with pink chopsticks and watched Tom's patio. The laborer loaded slabs of concrete onto his truck. He mopped his forehead with a blue bandana and slugged from a water bottle. Tom handed him a plate of tacos and a beer, probably buttering him up for a better deal.

That evening Mona stopped by. Mona still lived at Coco's old apartment house in Costa Mesa. It had been hours since the jackhammering, but Coco's nerves were jangled and her teeth hurt. She mixed a pitcher of dirty martinis, filled two pickle jars, and handed one to Mona. They sat on Coco's red faux leather sofa. Coco gave her the long version: Tom Fields-Jackson ran the table saw in his garage on Sundays and vacuumed late at night. The clean freak shampooed his rugs once a month with an eardrum-splitting carpet-cleaning machine; his juicer sounded like a jet engine; and when he exercised, he put Metallica songs on repeat on his phone and turned it up loud. To Coco's dismay, she could now recite James Hatfield lyrics in her sleep.

"He's driving me insane," Coco said.

"Is this just about noise? Invest in a good pair of earplugs."

Coco deliberated. "There *is* something else."

"What?"

Coco turned as demure as a kitten. "He doesn't like me very much."

"So? Everybody can't like you. Do you like him?"

"Not anymore. Well, maybe a little. Actually, he's pretty hot." Coco spoke in a little-girl voice, reminding herself of her mother baby-talking to her dad whenever she wanted a new ring or set of dishes.

"Maybe it's because your pheromones don't vibe." Mona pulled an olive off the toothpick, sucked out the pimento, and nibbled. "Don't take it personally." Mona held out her drink. They thudded jars.

Coco said, "Hmm."

"If it's really bugging you, we can fix it."

"It's all I can think about," Coco said. "But I can't get arrested again."

Coco already had two minor convictions—one for slamming a Roller Derby queen through a plate glass window at a rink the year before, and another for smashing a Roller Derby competitor's windshield with her skates. Another arrest could send her to prison.

Mona was Coco's most loyal friend—maybe her only friend. Coco loved being with her, even if she was a little bit envious. Mona was beautiful in that feline way men liked.

Tiny Man jumped onto the sofa and settled on Coco's lap. She cooed to him and scratched him under the chin, which got his engine going. She and Mona threw around ideas for getting back at her neighbor: spray-paint "honky geek" on his new pavers?

Break raw eggs into his mailbox? Dump used kitty litter onto his patio? No—those actions were crimes. More than getting back at him, she wanted him to notice her. One minute she liked him, the next she hated his guts.

"Tell me what else you know about him," Mona said.

"From his Facebook page," said Coco, "I know he works as a video game designer and his birthday is coming up."

"Any family?"

"A couple of cousins named Jake and Leonard were all I saw on his friends list."

Mona downed the rest of her martini, pressed her fingers to her temples, and, in a British accent, said, "I've got it!" What they would do began to crystallize, the pieces pixilating into place like Spock in a transporter on an old *Star Trek* episode.

"You'll need a wig," said Mona.

"I've got wigs up the ying-yang!" Coco said.

Coco scratched Tiny Man's left ear. "You love me, don't you?" She rubbed him under the chin. He gave her a look she interpreted as, "Yes, why yes, I do. There's no one else but you."

Sunday was his date night. Coco wondered if the same diminutive creature as last time would be over. She was so small she had to come from a hobbit clan. What on earth did he see in the Lilliputian? Coco looked forward to the fun; she could not resist making trouble, especially when it came to dealing with a scoundrel like Tom Fields-Jackson. She sang "Que sera sera, whatever will be will be."

He placed a red geranium in a clay pot on the faux Parisian table on the new slate patio no bigger than a T.J. Maxx fitting room. He was turning into Mr. Martha Stewart. He even strung white fairy lights around the perimeter of the patio. How romantic. How fucking quaint.

She turned the DIY channel to mute and listened to the clatter of his grill and the squeaky, lisping voice of the girlfriend as she arrived. She'd only seen blondes over there, usually short, but never this husky. *Spare me.*

Coco made a martini and took it upstairs to watch through the blinds. She raised her window so she could hear them. The lovebirds savored their wine as if they knew the difference between pinot and merlot. Tom cleared the table and brought out dessert.

"Ooo la la," the girlfriend said as he brought out what looked like chocolate mousse. Didn't he have anything better to do than fix fancy desserts? The mousse did look good from far away, not that the girlfriend needed one more ounce on her short, stocky frame. She already looked as if she might burst out of her blue-gray pantsuit. A juice cleanse and a heavy dose of probiotics would do her good. Tom lit up a joint and passed it to the girlfriend.

Coco raised her window a little more to catch a whiff. They had also moved onto mixed drinks. A pitcher of something orange-ish. Sangria? They swayed to Frank Sinatra. Same routine every Sunday eve. As predictable as dogs in heat, her father would say. Tom Fields-Jackson ground his skinny-ass groin into the girlfriend's belly region. Couldn't they go inside to act like canines?

Fields-Jackson stood six foot tall, just a few inches taller than Coco, the perfect height for her, while the pygmy was all of five feet. How did that work, a difference of a foot? It'd be like a Pekinese hooking up with a Great Dane. Whatever!

Tiny Man meowed at Coco's feet. She picked him up and carried him to the kitchen, where she spooned prescription cat food into a silver-plated bowl. Then she went to get ready. She had another drink and pulled on a strawberry blonde wig.

"Let the war begin."

In the clingy emerald-green dress she hadn't worn since her honeymoon four years ago, Coco stood outside Tom Fields-Jackson's gate. She carried a tote bag full of massage oils and candles.

In her breathiest, sexiest voice, Coco said, "Excuse me! Is this 102 Oak Path Aisle?" She daintily opened the gate.

Her question yanked Tom Fields-Jackson from his drunken and stoned dream state. "Can I help you?"

"I hope I'm not too late," she said. "They don't give me much traveling time between appointments."

Tom and the hydrant chick looked puzzled. Each appeared to wait for the other to explain Coco's presence because neither knew why she was there.

"Um, do I know you?" he said. "You look familiar."

Coco kept her cool and, in her sexiest voice, said, "Your cousin sent me. An early birthday gift."

"Jake?"

"He ordered massages for both of you," Coco said.

"Where do you know Jake from?"

"Gosh, we met so long ago. But tonight is about you two, so let's concentrate on having some fun."

Coco set her bag by the front door. "Tom, introduce me to your lovely friend."

"This is Freda," he said.

"I'm Tiffany," Coco said. "So glad to meet you."

Coco-Tiffany and Freda squeezed fingers.

"I'd love a drink." Coco eyed the pitcher.

"Of course." He refilled his and Freda's glasses too.

Another song by old Blue Eyes came on: "That's Life."

"Let's toast to your upcoming birthday," Coco said.

They *tink*ed glasses. Coco put down her glass and took Tom's right hand and Freda's left, and the three of them swayed in place.

Tom had that drunken squint, and Freda's ankle kept turning in, tipping her off her white kitten heels that matched the edging on her pantsuit.

The elf twitched back and forth to the music, her pudgy little cheeks flushed red. Freda clasped Coco's fingers with her child-size hand, but Coco let go to concentrate on Tom. She pressed up against him and sashayed the littlest bit. His eyelids hung at half-mast as he pressed against her.

Coco brought her mouth to his ear. "Ménage à trois?"

"Oh!" he choked out.

Behind Coco, Freda cleared her throat, trying to snag Tom's attention, but Tom was somewhere else now, getting into the music as Coco shimmied up and down his lean frame. Coco began to work his belt, and his skinny arms went up over his head, the way they must have as a little boy when his mother said, "Tommy, raise your arms so I can pull off your sweater."

Coco undid the top button of his jeans and was about to pull down the zipper when the girlfriend said, "Tom. *Tom?*"

When he didn't respond, Freda slung her purse strap over her fleshy shoulder and slurred, "I didn't think you were that kind of guy. I'm leaving."

"I *am* a good guy. Don't go." He started after her. Coco grabbed his arm.

"What about your massage, Tommy?"

He looked confused.

Freda blazed through the gate. Her heels grew faint as she tore down the path to the parking lot.

"Wouldn't we be more comfortable inside?" Coco said. Tom deliberated. "That was cool of Jake to book you."

"Aren't early birthday gifts the best?" Coco scrunched up her nose.

The interior of Tom Fields-Jackson's condo was all browns and blacks. He cued Aerosmith on his playlist. "Dream On," one of Coco's favorite songs, vibrated the walls.

He led her up the stairway to the bedroom, his phone in one hand, the bottle of Grey Goose in the other.

"This is one of those happy ending massages, isn't it?" He wrenched out of his skintight T-shirt, slugged from the vodka, and handed the bottle to her.

"One never knows, does one?" Coco said.

His bedroom was all IKEA: black dresser, black nightstands, black headboard.

"Is there rope?" Coco asked. "Or bandanas? I bet a guy like you has bandanas."

"For a massage?"

"A very special *type* of massage."

"So, it *is* the happy ending kind." He pulled open his top drawer and extracted a red and a blue bandana.

"Wait," she said. "I have just the thing." She found a roll of gray duct tape in her tote. "We'll use this instead."

She pushed him onto the bed, kicked off her heels, and tossed the duct tape into the air.

"May I?" She held out the roll.

"Why not?" he said.

She ripped off lengths and fastened his wrists to the wooden posts of the lightweight headboard. She felt in her pocket for the Molly capsules Mona had given her.

He laughed and said, "What's your business called, Fifty Yards of Gray Duct Tape Massage?"

She laughed.

"You look like somebody," he mumbled. "I like your hair." He tried to reach out to touch it, but his hand was duct taped to the headboard.

Coco fingered her wig.

"C'mon. Join me." He moved his arm as if he could tap the mattress, but he could only wiggle his fingers dangling from the duct tape wrap.

"I have something for us." She showed him the capsules in her hand. "Molly. Open up." She poured vodka into an empty water glass on the nightstand and held the glass to his lips.

He swallowed and gazed bleary-eyed at her. Vodka dribbled down his chin, which she dabbed off with her finger.

She played with the top button of her blouse and unbuttoned it. She danced to another Aerosmith song as she dropped the blouse.

Downstairs the metal gate clanged and there was a pounding on the door.

"Tom? Tom, you up there?" Freda called as she pressed the doorbell. "My car won't start. Your screen door's locked. Tom!"

"That Freda?" He went to get up but couldn't.

The gate clanged again.

Coco gave him a conciliatory look, bent down, and kissed him hard. Their tongues tangled.

"She was too short for me, anyway," he mumbled. "Why haven't we met before?"

"We have!" She pulled off her wig.

He took in a sharp breath, fluttered his eyelids, and conked out.

"Tom?" She shook his shoulders.

He wouldn't wake up.

"Shit," she said. *Just my luck.* Was he dead?

She pressed her ear to his chest. Aerosmith was still blaring, making it hard to hear. She jumped up, backed toward the bathroom, and, with a towel from the vanity, wiped down wherever she'd been. She pulled on her blouse, used his finger to unlock his phone, and called 9-1-1. She grabbed the bottle of vodka and went downstairs, using some of the alcohol on a towel to wipe down the banister and doorknobs. She went out the back in case Freda was lurking on the patio.

At home, Coco poured another drink and fed treats to Tiny Man. The sirens were closing in. She'd wiped off the phone, hadn't she? She could only hope. She didn't want him to die, God no. But she did look forward to sleeping in for the first time in months, and she imagined Tiny Man did too.

SANDMAN

Inspired by *M*, Fritz Lang's 1931 film

A plume of smoke erupted over Saddleback Mountain as Sherry walked Edie to school. Edie pointed. "Look, Mommy, a wicked genie," and it did look like one, a mean one, emerging from a brass lamp. Sherry brushed ashes as large as cornflakes from her daughter's mop of curls. At least twenty fires blazed along the length of the state. How was that possible? California was on fire, and the idea of it made Sherry's stomach churn.

They reached the playground just as the kids lined up for flag deck, a tradition the elementary school began ten years ago. Edie asked her mother if she could walk home with Dana and Senna, and without giving it much thought, Sherry said yes. Edie ran across the faint layer of ash dusting the blacktop to stand with her third-grade class. Dark clouds from another fire south trundled across the sky, ominous and threatening.

Sherry joined a gaggle of moms huddled under the oak tree in the corner of the playground. "Did you hear?" one mom said. "A boy in Costa Mesa is missing."

"Missing?" said Sherry. "What do you mean *missing*?"

Orange County, equidistant between L.A. and San Diego, was supposed to be a safe place, as far as safe places went, but hearing about a missing kid anywhere made her shudder. The principal called the group to order, and teachers, children, and parents covered their hearts with their hands and said the Pledge of Allegiance. The principal, usually smiley to the point of absurdity, wore a strained expression as she made a few general announcements. Did she have information about the boy? Flag deck ended and everyone walked to their classrooms, but the moms remained.

"What do they think happened to him?" asked Sherry.

"They're not saying," said a mom.

"They don't want to freak everyone out, but I bet they know," said another.

The group went quiet. Sherry imagined that each of them was considering her own children and how often she let them walk alone to a friend's or home from school. Sherry didn't want to be a helicopter parent. She wanted to foster independence, and the best way to do that was to trust Edie to do simple things. Theirs was a seemingly safe neighborhood, but who knew for sure? Sherry remembered reading that one in a hundred was a sociopath, which meant in their beach community of thirteen thousand, one hundred and thirty were sociopaths. A few to every street? It was too much to take in. And what percentage were psychopaths? She had to stop thinking this way.

Sherry couldn't stand here talking because it only made her dread the worst. She was the only single parent among them and had to get back to her office. She needed to drum up clients for her coaching business. Rent was coming due, and her ex had proved himself a deadbeat dad. She said goodbye to the group and hurried home.

Sherry had a Zoom call with a client at nine, so she cut through the park and hurried past neighbors walking their white puffballs and rangy retrievers. Construction workers were putting up another starter castle, as if her beach town needed one more.

At home she poured a tepid cup of coffee and logged onto Zoom. After that appointment, there was another, then another, and the busy day with potential clients took her mind off the missing boy until three o'clock, when Edie was due home. She poured a glass of water and went out front to sit in the sun and wait.

Sherry heard Dana and Senna's loud voices and walked down to the gate to greet the children. There was no Edie. The kids, caught up in their own antics, didn't look over at Sherry. They were almost past the house when Sherry said, "Where's Edie?"

The kids stopped in their tracks. Senna pivoted and looked confused. "I don't know."

"You don't know?"

"She left with us but then she disappeared."

"Disappeared? Why didn't you look for her?"

"I don't know. We thought maybe you picked her up."

Sherry ran inside and called the moms. No one had seen her daughter. She called the school, which was on speed dial. *Was Edie still there? Did something happen? Could someone take a look?*

No one knew anything, and there were no kids left on the property as far as Mina, in the front office, knew.

Sherry felt dizzy. Why did she even say Edie could walk home with her friends, especially after hearing about the missing boy? Her daughter was only in third grade and small for her age. Sherry would enroll Edie in a self-defense class at once. The boy who disappeared lived one town over, far enough away not to worry danger was at hand yet close enough to worry it might be.

Her daughter knew to come right home after school. She knew not to talk to strangers. The sun felt hot on Sherry's shoulders. The sound of the construction workers up the street pounding nails into wood felt like the nails were being drilled into her skull. She grabbed her phone and car keys and ran out to her minivan. Surely her daughter had to be somewhere close.

The school parking lot had emptied out. She pulled into the No Parking zone and ran inside. Mina at the front desk said they'd searched the school, but Edie was nowhere to be found.

Sherry jumped back in the van and drove the streets. Whenever she saw kids on the sidewalk, she stopped and asked about Edie. The kids didn't know her; their school had a lot of students, and each grade was fairly self-contained. Some of the kids looked at her with an expression that said *who is this strange woman?*

After she drove up and down every street, she pulled into her driveway, walked to the front porch, and there she was, her Edie, on the recliner, knees pulled up to her chin.

"Where the hell were you? I looked all over. Why didn't you do what you said you were going to do?" Sherry yanked her off the chair and hugged her so hard Edie said, "Ouch." She let her go. Edie flopped back down onto the chair.

"I was at the park. I played on the swings."

"You're never walking home with friends again, missy. How am I supposed to trust you if you don't keep your word?"

"I'm sorry!"

The park was the one place Sherry hadn't looked. She shook her finger at Edie. "Never ever do that again."

"I'm sorry, Mommy!"

Sherry collapsed onto the swing. She looked at her phone. Four o'clock. She'd spent an hour looking for Edie, but it felt like days. "What do you say we have a pizza and salad delivered?" she said. "I have no energy to make dinner."

Edie clapped her hands. "I love pizza!"

Fifteen of the twenty fires ablaze throughout the state were still uncontained. The word itself, "uncontained," made Sherry tremble. Some years ago, a fire threatened to descend the hills and invade her neighborhood. From their yard, Sherry had seen the glow a couple of miles away, yet the blaze was still too close for comfort. She and her then-husband packed the car with their computers, a box of pictures, two suitcases stuffed with clothes, their passports, and as much of their food as they could fit in the car, and were ready to go, but at the last minute the wind sent the fire in the opposite direction, and they were spared.

Now what made the stress of the missing boy worse was the unrelenting heat. Ninety degrees during the day was unheard of by the beach, but the thermometer didn't lie. Being beach dwellers, they were among the residents who didn't have air conditioners and depended on fans and open windows to cool off.

On the porch Sherry and Edie ate cheese pizza and salad, then Sherry helped her with homework. Edie watched TV for an hour and then was upstairs and off to bed. Sherry hauled a fan into Edie's room and opened the window. Edie wore a light T-shirt and undies to sleep in. It was too hot for anything more. Sherry kissed her goodnight and left the door open a crack.

She went online to search for news about the missing boy. He hadn't been found, and now the media had given the perpetrator the name *Sandman* because it was thought the boy had been snatched while he slept.

Then Sherry googled missing children. The statistics were stunning. In 2019 alone, 421,394 children in the U.S. were reported missing. Most were located. Only one out of every ten thousand was found dead, but still . . . to have to go through the trauma of your kid being missing was unbearable. In the UK, 112,835 children were reported missing each year, which equated to one in two hundred. Hundreds of thousands went missing in India, China, and Africa, and many were never found. Sherry had to stop reading. She x-ed out of the site and slammed down the lid of her laptop.

She thought she should tell the moms that Edie had come home, but didn't want to call each one, so she posted a photo she had of Edie on their front porch with the caption, "She made it home." She included happy face emojis. No sooner had she posted than moms responded with hearts and likes.

Sherry poured a glass of pinot with the hope the wine would calm her down. She went out on the front porch into the balmy night, but the soundtrack of sirens didn't help. Police car sirens, fire truck sirens. September had never been so hot or so loud. Sweat trickled down the sides of her face. Her next-door neighbors, Madeline and Rook, were out, too, and when they saw her, they invited Sherry over.

"I better not," she said, thinking of her daughter upstairs.

"Just one little drinky-poo," said Madeline.

"Why don't you come over here?"

Her neighbors picked up their wineglasses and joined her on the porch. They talked about the missing boy, what might have happened—a runaway? Parent abduction?—and moved on to Sherry's woes about being a good mom.

"Maybe I should've given Edie's dad another chance. Then she'd have two parents looking after her, keeping her safe from this bastard."

"He cheated on you," Madeline said.

"There are worse things, right?" Sherry swirled her glass of wine.

"Are there?"

"Maybe I work too much. I could be a better mom."

"You're a great mom," said Rook. "Have you taken your ex to court to force him to pay child support?"

"I can't afford a lawyer!" Sherry went on as she did when she drank, and her neighbors commiserated. Two glasses of wine later, they called it a night. Sherry made sure the back door was locked and went upstairs. Edie was splayed out across the bed, the sheet kicked to the floor. What a beautiful sight. She thought of the mother missing her son and his empty bed. Sherry could not imagine such an absence.

A shower would feel good, but she didn't think she had the energy, so she splashed water on her face, brushed her teeth, and not more than a minute after her head hit the pillow, she was in dreamland.

A week later at flag deck, Sherry joined the moms frantically abuzz about the one parent missing from the pack.

"Her little Jolene is gone," a mom said.

"Gone?" said Sherry.

"She wasn't in her bed when Mary went to wake her for school. The police are looking for her."

The Sandman's work?

Sherry felt a wave of heat. The humidity had lifted, but the heatwave that washed through her was the heat of fear, the worry that danger was coming close, circling their town, sniffing her ankles. Across the playground the kids had lined up, and there was Edie, laughing with her friends.

Sherry remembered pictures Jolene's mom had posted of her daughter on Instagram—in her soccer uniform up at the field, in her bathing suit at the community pool, in their yard at her birthday party. She texted Mary to see if there was anything she could do, but Mary didn't respond.

All week long, Sherry felt like she had a low-grade fever. It was from stress, that much was obvious. She felt this way when she'd caught her husband cheating on her, which she discovered by affixing a tracking device to his car. She told herself she was glad he was gone.

Two tense weeks went by, and the boy didn't turn up, nor did Jolene. Authorities reminded parents to keep watch of their kids. But Sherry believed they themselves were safe. Their bedrooms were on the second story, and there was no way anyone could get in. No tree branches leaning against the side of the house, no patio or terrace to climb onto.

∾

She went to wake up Edie for school, and she wasn't there. The devil had circled and landed at her house. The window was wide open. The screen had been cut out. A ladder leaned against the clapboards. Sherry felt like her head was going to explode. She called the police, and moments later sirens blared.

Madeline sat with Sherry while the police asked questions. When they learned Madeline was the next-door neighbor, they questioned her, too. Anyone strange hanging around? Anything she noticed?

She couldn't help them.

Anything out of the ordinary? Unusual delivery people, unfamiliar faces in the neighborhood, anything that struck a wrong chord?

Sorry, nothing, she was sad to say.

Edie's backpack sat by the front door. Would she ever go to school again? Sherry couldn't bear the thought that she wouldn't. She could hardly think straight, but something kept bugging her. Was there anything the kidnapped kids had in common? Two went to the same school but not the boy. Two lived in her beach community but not the boy.

Instagram. Was the boy on Instagram? She called the police officer who'd given her his card and asked if he'd put her in touch with the boy's mother. He said he'd pass on Sherry's number and email to the mom.

Two hours later the mother of the boy called. Sherry invited her over, along with Mary and the rest of the moms from school who continually texted and called and a few of the dads. The parents had to do something; the police were having no luck.

It was as Sherry thought: the one thing the missing children had in common was their parents' posting pictures of them on Instagram. Of course. It was a perfect place for predators to find subjects. Her precious Edie. What had Sherry done? She only meant to share the photo of her daughter's return with her mom friends. She didn't post pictures for creeps. She forgot that she never changed her account to private though she'd been reminded hundreds of times and had so many followers at this point she lost track of the amount of randoms that followed her.

She couldn't eat. She couldn't sleep. Something good had to come out of this. They'd lay a trap. One of the moms offered to be the guinea pig and posted photos of her little Lara. Better than that, she took the photo near their house number along with a photo of the house and in the caption even mentioned the name of their beach hamlet. They formed small groups, and every night the parents kept watch. They checked their Ring cameras, but no one saw a thing.

It had been five days and Sherry was losing hope. Maybe the Sandman had moved on. He might have migrated to another town, another county, another state. Or he may have quit his evil ways. Did serial killers ever hang it up and find something less hateful to do with their time?

Moms and dads, plus Sherry's neighbors Madeline and Rook, surrounded the house in cars, bushes, and one sat in the child's closet, waiting. They all had their phones at the ready, all in silent mode, as well as pepper spray, baseball bats, and kitchen knives. But no guns. They all promised not to bring guns.

At one in the morning, a strange SUV pulled up in front of the house and turned off the engine. The SUV sat at the curb, but no one got out. The parents went on high alert. This had to be him.

"What's he waiting for?" Sherry said to Madeline, who sat in Sherry's darkened minivan a few cars back from where the SUV parked.

And then the SUV started up, and its terrible screeching fan belt echoed in the night. Madeline grabbed Sherry's wrist. "That sound," Madeline said. "I heard that the night Edie went missing."

Sherry texted the group. "We're following the SUV!"

They waited for him to go around the corner, then pulled into the street. On the way, Madeline called the police, who said a screeching fan belt wasn't enough evidence to arrest someone.

"But he might have my daughter!" Sherry said on speakerphone. She was beside herself but didn't want to let the SUV out of her sight.

"I'm sorry, ma'am, it's just not enough."

Madeline hit End and said, "What are we going to do?"

He got on the freeway and headed inland. Twenty minutes later he parked in the driveway of an old house on the historic side of town. Sherry reached into the console, looking for gum, mints, anything to dull the sour taste in her mouth, and came across the tracker. Ah, the famous tracking device that she'd affixed to her then-husband's car. She held it up.

"Be right back," she said, and snuck off in the dark to his SUV. Then she crept up to the window that wasn't covered with drapes and peeked. There he was, feeding a cat, dropping a slice of white bread into the toaster, looking through mail. She returned to the van, but not before placing the magnetized tracking device behind the bumper.

The next evening the device's continuous beeping woke up Sherry, who rallied the parents. He was on the move. The parents mobilized and followed Sherry, who tracked his SUV to the Ortega Highway in South Orange County. The highway lead to Lake Elsinore over the mountain. There were few homes in those hills. A fire was reported to be growing up the mountain. Sherry parked behind what was likely his SUV, and the others followed suit.

"That's the car!" Sherry tripped over rocks and righted herself before she fell. Her heart raced; her mouth went dry.

Rook pierced holes in two of the tires so they'd deflate. The parents set out through the woods, following a path worn down by someone, most likely the killer. The trees grew sparse; the orange sky bled through. The smell of fire stung Sherry's nose.

In the clearing, Madeline pointed and said, "There he is!"

The figure on the cliff must have heard her because he turned his head lizard-fast. The moms and dads approached but stopped twenty feet away. He looked out over the crevasse, as if wondering if he could escape the crowd, then pivoted and faced them.

"He's the Sandman?" Sherry said to no one in particular. He looked so harmless. Pudgy, with a baby face. She'd expected someone imposing, disfigured.

"Hey creep," said Jolene's dad, Ted, who rushed him and grabbed his arm.

"What do you want from me?" the Sandman said, trying to jerk his arm away.

"My daughter," Sherry growled. "You bastard."

Parents called out taunts, threats.

"You don't deserve to live," called a mom.

"What have you done with Edie?" Sherry's voice had a shrill edge.

"Edie?" he said, and let her name linger in his mouth.

Sherry stood a foot away from him, saw the dark circles under his eyes, his gray teeth. She saw him as a little boy, unloved, hurt by the people who were supposed to care for him, and for a moment felt sorry for him. But only for a moment. "You've given me my worst nightmare."

The Sandman looked horrified. "I—" he began, and didn't finish.

Ted squeezed his arm so hard the Sandman called out. "Help!"

The parents spread in a semicircle to block him should he try to get away.

Ted squeezed his throat. Sherry gripped Ted's arm. "We should call the police."

"I just did." Rook held up his phone.

She wanted the creep dead, but prison would be worse. Convicts hated dudes who preyed on children. They'd give him his due.

The Sandman made gurgling noises. Ted dropped his hand from the Sandman's neck but remained poised to react.

"Kill the bastard," a mom said. "If we let him go, the courts will find a loophole and he'll be back on the street."

"I didn't do a thing." The Sandman was all innocence. "Let me go!"

"He should die," someone said.

"*You* killed your children," the Sandman said. "It's *your* fault! All those pictures of your precious darlings. It's like you're saying here, take them, they're yours."

"Why are we letting him live?" a dad said, and rushed toward him, and the others joined in.

The Sandman screamed and started to run but there was nowhere to go, and he ran right off the cliff, his arms spread wide against the unearthly orange glow of the fire in the moonless night. Sherry gasped and looked over the edge. Far below, in the smoky haze, the Sandman landed on a jagged boulder, his body askew, impaled by the rock's pointy tip.

ROWBOAT

The sky was black as Nina rowed past the Fun Zone. Fairy lights stretched over restaurant patios, and the Ferris wheel that had been there for decades spun about, its rickety bench seats looking like they'd snap right off should a strong wind blow in off the ocean.

Nina liked being out on the water at night. By then most of the tourists who clotted the bay since sunrise with rented eight-person canopy-covered Duffy boats had retreated to their hotel rooms, burrowed in at a bayside bar, or rode the ferry to Balboa Island, where forty-three hundred residents and a few blocks of shops—ice cream and frozen banana stands, restaurants, boutiques—packed its .2-square-mile radius, leaving the bay to the party boats and to her and her rowboat, *Jailbird*.

She loved the salty and dank-smelling night. The water was like glass. The boat had no running lights, which could garner a fine from the harbor patrol, if they wanted to get picky, but money was tight. Most of Nina's income from typing up medical reports went to paying back the money she'd embezzled, so on moonless nights like this, she was super vigilant lest she get run over by a yacht. Roland, her last boyfriend, had a vintage muscle car he sped around town in, but he refused to go boating. She could put her own life at risk, he said, but he wasn't about to get run over by a party boat.

Bridges and a ferry connected Newport Harbor's eight mostly residential islands. Out on the water, traversing the narrow canals, gliding beneath overpasses, Nina imagined what Venice felt like— not that she'd ever get to Italy. After she had served a year in CIW (California Institute for Women), she was lucky to return to Newport Beach, with its palm trees, surfers, and the book club she'd been a part of before she was sent away. In prison, reading was the only thing that had kept her sane.

She rowed toward Celine's house down by the harbor. Lovely book club member, that Celine. It had been two weeks since the last book club, but the wound remained fresh. In front of everyone, Celine had made fun of her for being a convicted felon.

"You'd have to be a dunce to get caught embezzling," Celine said. Everyone had laughed, and one member, Jackie, who always hosted in her big oceanfront house, nervously changed the subject to her impending first Botox appointment and her worry that the treatment might freeze her face in an unpleasant expression instead of taking the wrinkles away.

Nina held a grudge against Celine, which only grew worse. Nina's boss, Jimmy Toldano, made zillions by peddling knockoff jewelry and purses. If only he'd given her the raise she asked for, Nina wouldn't have had to embezzle him. What's worse, Celine had been a friend before prison, yet the year Nina was away, Celine was the one book club member who never visited, never wrote a letter, never even sent a book.

But that night two weeks ago Celine went on and on, joking that Nina was their first trailer trash club member. Of course, she was kidding, of course! Yet the comment cut deep. Nina hoped Celine would apologize, but she never did, even though she could see how much she had affected Nina.

Nina talked about her festering hurt feelings to her parole officer, Jamie Lerner. "She never said she was sorry," Nina whined.

"Some people aren't good at sorry," Lerner said. "You need to find a way to deal with frustrations. They're part of life."

"At night I go out onto the water and row," Nina said.

"Rowing is great exercise," Lerner said, "and a healthy way to deal with your frustrations, but is it wise to row at night? You could get run over by a yacht."

"I'm careful."

"It's that temper of yours that really concerns me," Lerner said. "Remember to always, *always,* count to ten. Better yet, count in Spanish; it takes longer."

A three-story yacht blasting disco glided by, rocking *Jailbird.* Nina held onto the sides and gazed into the inky water. If she fell in, she'd survive. The bay wasn't more than twenty feet at its deepest point, and she was fewer than fifty feet from shore. You'd have to be an idiot to live by the bay and not know how to swim.

At the last book club meeting, Celine said she was taking swimming lessons, now that she lived beside the water, but she wasn't making progress. She hated getting wet. Brilliant.

As Nina reached Celine's bayside home, inherited from her parents, she stopped rowing but drifted in the outgoing tide. Celine's house had floor-to-ceiling windows. At night when the interior was lit up, it was like peering into a life-size diorama. Nina had rowed by the house many times, especially since the night Celine was mean to her. The blinds were never drawn. Exhibitionists liked to be watched, and prowlers liked watching. Nina knew a few in CIW who would love these curtainless bayside homes.

Tonight, Celine was with someone. A man. Nina raised the binoculars she kept in the boat because you never knew when there was something you needed to see up close. Celine poured wine into the man's glass. Roland's glass. Roland? They toasted. Celine held her baby finger aloft. Didn't she know it was déclassé, raising your pinkie when you consumed wine or tea? Nina wanted to bite it off and feed it to the fishes.

Nina had introduced Celine to Roland at the book club's holiday party right before she caught him cheating on her. She learned through Instagram of all things. The idiot had let his other squeeze take selfies, which the stupid girl posted.

Roland had a great kitchen where he'd made fresh pasta for Nina, and madeleines even, but he had a bad habit of spitting and had an eye tic that acted up when he was nervous. Nina was willing to overlook his nerves and filthy habits, but she couldn't forgive his cheating. Yet now that Celine was with her old blinking, pacing, and spitting boyfriend, Nina had second thoughts. What was up with that?

Lerner's voice was in her head. *Count to ten.* Uno, dos, tres....

Nina wasn't pining for the jerk; he'd served his purpose. After she was paroled, he helped pass the time as she acclimated to life without iron bars. He was also good in bed. But he wanted some say in how she dressed and what lipstick she wore. Freak! He even wanted her to get a boob job. She said she'd get a boob job if he got a penile implant, and he had the nerve to be insulted.

She felt like screaming, but out here on the bay, near the boardwalk where a few pedestrians strolled about, screaming was a bad idea. She breathed in the briny night air, reminded herself she was lucky to be back in Newport and no longer in her cement cubicle. She rowed home fast and screamed into her pillow.

The next night, Saturday, Nina went out on the boat again. The air smelled fishy and moist and made her skin feel soft. She promised herself she wouldn't do it, but she couldn't help herself: she rowed to Celine's. And there they were, Roland and Celine, swilling wine from long-stemmed glasses, kissing and slobbering all over one another. *Close your damn curtains.* Nina had to do something.

Quatro, cinco, seis….

Book club was coming up that weekend. She didn't want to go, but she agreed to bring dessert.

She went to Target—Targét to her—to buy cupcakes. Rubicon cupcakes were the best, short of baking them yourself. She would bring a cupcake for each member to take home in their own miniature pink box with their names calligraphied with a black Sharpie. Yes, that would be perfect.

Nina found the laxative capsules she was looking for in the pharmacy aisle. She'd inject the powder into Celine's cupcake. The results would be harmless but annoying. Then, for some odd reason she found herself on the pesticide aisle—kismet? Or was it that old song, "Strychnine," by The Sonics roaming her brain? Rat poison. She'd inject only a smidge into the cupcake, just enough to make Celine sick but not kill her. She'd wait till after dessert was served before she injected it into Celine's boxed cupcake. And if at dinner Celine apologized for being so mean, then, of course, she wouldn't do it at all.

The following Sunday night the book group met on a member's patIo to discuss *Anna Karenina*. Nina sat beside Celine, ready to give her every opportunity to apologize. Most of the women empathized with Anna and understood how distraught she must have felt after Vronsky's rejection, but not Celine.

"What a weak-kneed, lily-livered excuse for a human being. Get over it, Anna!" she said, making everyone laugh. Celine could be a stand-up if she wanted.

The group dined on a grape-and-cheese charcuterie, stuffed peppers, a green salad with pomegranate seeds that got stuck in your teeth, and wine—lots of wine. And cupcakes.

As the group on the patio enjoyed dessert and opened another bottle, Nina excused herself to use the restroom. Kramer, the resident border collie, who sat by her feet when she was eating, followed her inside. Instead of going to the bathroom, Nina headed for the pink boxes. Kramer must have known something was up because he kept dropping a red ball at her feet. Nina threw the ball and shuffled through the boxes until she found the cupcake box with Celine's name. She was about to inject the confection with rat poison when Kramer dropped the ball on her foot and whimpered. She looked into his eyes and seemed to catch the message he was sending: what if someone other than Celine ate the cupcake?

"Who *are* you?" she asked Kramer, closed the box, and threw the ball in frustration.

The next night Nina rowed to the center of the bay. The air smelled of seaweed and salt. The water was rough from a storm brewing that bucked the boat like a pony. Fifty yards out, a ferry holding three cars and a flock of pedestrians heading for Balboa Island crossed. Might the wake be strong enough to capsize the boat? She wasn't worried about herself because she knew how to swim.

Nina had invited Celine because she thought: captive audience! And to her surprise, Celine had accepted. Now Nina would make Celine understand how upset her comments had made her. She needed to excise these dark thoughts of revenge from her mind. Celine was human, wasn't she? Somehow, Nina would convince her to say she was sorry.

The sky was a peachy pink as a dozen party boats loitered on the water. A few bloated yachts two- and three-stories high blasted disco and kicked up waves, rocking her tiny boat. She rowed to Celine's bayside home a quarter mile south where she waited on the dock. Celine waved eagerly, and Nina threw her the line. Celine caught it and wrapped the line around a cleat. Then she handed Nina a two-person cooler and tossed a canvas bag crinkly with snacks. Finally, Celine stepped in, tipping the boat, making her gasp. Water sloshed over the gunwales. Celine was a big girl—top heavy, she liked to say about herself with a grin.

"I can't swim," Celine said, and settled on the low bench.

"Don't worry," Nina said. "We won't be too far from shore, and it's not that deep. And there's a life preserver under there." She pointed at the bench.

With the oar, Nina directed *Jailbird* close to the mooring and freed the line.

The sky was now the color of a three-day-old bruise. The incoming tide made it difficult to navigate the rowboat. From the top of the tote bag, Celine produced a candle.

"Vanilla." She set the small metal votive on the bench beside her and lit it.

Fifty feet away Fleetwood Mac blasted from the speakers of a Newport party yacht that jiggled the rowboat as it glided by. Celine held on. A fishy smelling wind blew in.

Celine reached into the cooler and withdrew a bottle of wine and two stemmed wineglasses.

"Glass can be dangerous on a boat," Nina said.

"Would you rather I put them away? You know I like to live dangerously." Celine winked.

"No, it's all right, this time."

Celine always brought the best wine to book club.

The boat drifted.

Celine poured and they toasted, but instead of Nina feeling of good cheer, that image of Celine and Roland bloomed before her, and she felt steamed all over again.

"I've been thinking," Nina said, preparing to talk about the bad vibes between them and wanting to discuss the matter like mature human beings.

But Celine interrupted.

"What was it like in there?" she asked. "Do you miss anything about it?"

"Seriously?" Nina said.

"I bet there's something," Celine said in a singsong voice.

"Oh, yeah, I miss the food. Five-star dining every night. You'd love it." Nina's jaw hurt. Stress made her clench. She took up the oars and rowed toward the center of the bay.

"Should you be doing that?" Celine said, no longer singsongy. "That yacht is headed straight for us." She gulped the rest of her wine.

"You like to live dangerously, right?" Nina wore a devilish grin.

By now the yacht was maybe ten feet away, and the Lilliputian rowboat rocked wildly from the swells just as Celine stood up to wave at the partygoers. A swell jogged the boat sharply, and Celine toppled backward into the water. Her glass went flying, and her mouth made an O, green eyes awestruck. Her back hit the bay. Nina could not believe her good fortune. Celine flapped her arms, trying to keep her face above the water. The partiers were oblivious to what was going on down below.

If I wanted to, I could push her head down with the oar.

Poor Celine flung her arms about like an octopus.

"Stop thrashing already," Nina yelled.

"Help me!"

The bay was cold, and Nina hated swimming at night. There was no telling what was in the dark water that might sting or take a bite. No way was she jumping in, and she didn't want to watch her drown after all, so she threw Celine the life preserver and, with great reluctance, pulled her to the boat.

"Put your hands here," Nina said, placing them on the side. "Now try hefting yourself in." Celine's big boobs kept catching but finally she made it. She looked so pitiful with her hair smooshed flat against her skull like a wet dog's.

"I thought I was going to drown out there," Celine said, wringing the bay water from her hair. Her eyelids fluttered with recognition. "You *wanted* me to drown, didn't you?"

"Of course not," Nina said half-heartedly.

Just then the Tiki Boat, a two-story party boat, glided past. The Allman Brothers's "Whipping Post" played at top volume.

Nina gave Celine her jacket—her teeth were chattering. A party boat passing the other way blasted "YMCA," with the partiers dancing, making letter shapes with their arms.

As the rowboat aimed for the Fun Zone, the ferry crossed in front of them and someone who looked just like Roland leaned on the railing with a woman in pink. The way his arm was around her, this was no relative.

"Oh my God," Celine said.

"What?"

Celine pointed. "The bastard. We have a date for later. He said he was working till ten."

"You used to make fun of him when we were dating."

"I know I did but then, shit, I fell for the asshole." Celine's eyes looked moist. She held a hand over her quivering mouth. "And he's really good in bed."

"Yes, I know," Nina said, dryly.

Celine shook her head. "I should kill the bastard."

"Men have died for less."

Celine pursed her lips. "You'll help me, right? You probably know how to get away with murder. Isn't that what they teach you in prison? How should we do it?"

"You can't be serious," Nina said.

"Serious as a heart attack," Celine said.

They rowed to Celine's mooring. Nina jumped out, roped the boat to the buoy, and Celine climbed onto the dock.

Nina said she'd be glad to help, but this time she'd make damn sure it went wrong. That would be apology enough.

SEA CHANGE

Captain settled on the beach towel against Emily's legs. The Dalmatian smelled like fresh croissants, something baked, buttery, warm. Luke used to bring her pastries on their mornings together. He checked into the police station, then said he was on his way to talk to a witness or investigate a suspect, slip out the door, and drive to her apartment two blocks from the harbor.

Emily had met Luke on this beach eleven months ago to this very day. Captain and she were playing Frisbee, and Luke, in the Frisbee's path, caught the faded red disk and spun it back to Emily.

She was still crazy about the man, damn him, so she visited this spot on the first of the month in case he showed up. He said he would. Luke was in his fifties, fifteen years older than Emily. Dark eyelashes mobbed his green eyes. His wavy hair, the color of oxidized silver, was cut short and neat. His loquacity was a refreshing change from her husband, Stephen, who preferred silence or music to talking. Luke could go on and on about books and movies and said more than "I liked it" or "it stunk." Luke talked about the criminals he dealt with at the police station, which fascinated her. He even made dry rot—he worked with wood to relax—sound compelling.

She sat up on the beach towel. Skim boarders with bodies like twisted rubber navigated the sand-slicked shore, dodging a couple in big straw hats and sunglasses.

A young woman sprinted along the glaring shoreline, brown ponytail bouncing behind her. She reminded Emily of the girl she once was, so unencumbered, jogging along the shoreline, the world her oyster, as her father liked to say. At twenty, Emily's friends called her Miss Hopeful. Now, closer to forty than to thirty, she looked for answers that came in the form of omens. A new bloom on the African violet foreshadowed a new friendship while a broken water glass meant she'd soon fight with a friend.

Being with Luke made her feel young. He didn't dwell on his marriage woes, but he did say his wife, Connie, made him recycle old greeting cards. She kept cards they exchanged over the years in a shoebox in the pantry. Why buy new cards when they had perfectly good ones to reuse, was her rationale.

Emily had never heard of anyone having an affair over a spouse's frugality, but apparently this annoyed Luke because he brought Emily sappy Hallmark tomes from Rite Aid every time he came over. They weren't her usual style, but she coveted them because they were from him.

Falling in love was as random and as unlikely as finding a peach pit in an apple pie. Luke's easy way with words and cheesy cards nudged Emily from her quiet and lonely but stable life with Stephen into an unpredictable yet colorful realm with Luke.

On the beach towel, Captain nestled in closer. "You know me, don't you?" she said, kissing the top of his sleek spotted head. "You miss him too."

These days it was just her and her dog. Dogs didn't let you down.

Teenagers kicked a volleyball back and forth across the sand behind them. A low growl issued from the back of Captain's throat as the kids moved down the shoreline. One ginger-haired boy glanced back, looking worried as if Captain might chase them. But Captain was more interested in the sun. He stared at it as if it were a place he longed for. Emily tried to break him of the habit; he was only four and growing cataracts. She bought him Doggles doggie sunglasses, but he hated the elasticized band clasping his boxy head, pawed them off, and hid every pair until she gave up and stopped buying them.

A lone figure a quarter mile down the shoreline strolled toward them. He was tall like Luke and swung his arms the same way, with a come-what-may attitude.

It would be just like Luke to remember their eleven-month anniversary and turn up on the beach. He always celebrated moments.

"Keep this on your balcony," he said on their two-month anniversary when he brought her an oleander seedling from a hedge at home. "When you look at it, think of me."

"Oleanders are poisonous," she said.

"Only if you eat them."

"Your wife gets the hedge," Emily said. "I get a potted plant."

He pulled her onto his lap. "I can't leave my kids."

"But they're grown," she said, so low he had to lean in to hear. "They're away at college." She hated herself for talking like this.

"They come home on breaks." His voice had a pleading quality. "But you're right, they're grown. What do they need me for?"

"No, no, I'm sorry." She understood. She would feel the same if she and Stephen had kids.

Maybe it was a blessing that Luke was out of her life now. If it had worked out, he could never give her babies. He already had two kids, which Connie said was enough and made him get his tube snipped or whatever it was they did to men.

At one time Stephen had wanted a family. They were still making love then and tried, but nothing took. She was sure he'd been more in love with his yoga practice and students than he was with her. He could go days at a time without talking because of his vow of silence. On his silent days, the quiet in their cottage was deafening. Stephen and she would communicate via Post-It notes. The first day was the hardest.

"What do you want for dinner?" Emily would throw open the fridge, forgetting as she hunkered down to search the freezer drawer that he wasn't talking.

When he didn't respond, she asked again. Still nothing.

He tapped the table and held up a small wood-rimmed blackboard he bought at a toy store.

"Stir fry?" He illustrated his question with a happy face.

"I'm going to scream," she said, "in your ear."

He nodded at her and flashed her the peace sign.

Five months into Emily and Luke's friendship—it was nothing more at that point—Stephen went to India for his annual month-long yoga retreat. Emily usually went with him, but this year she told him to go without her, that she needed to declutter the house, catch up on her reading, spend time with her sister.

On the day Stephen flew out of LAX, Luke came over with a lily-of-the-valley seedling in a green ceramic frog.

"You know the real me," he said, and swooped her up in his big beefy arms and carried her to the second bedroom that served as her office. She opened the futon. They piled their clothes on her office chair. Luke set his holster on top of the pile, and they made love for the first time. Captain sat outside the office door and whimpered.

As they lay there recovering, Luke laughed and said, "My heart is beating like crazy."

"Are you okay?" It was common knowledge older men died while having sex, not that he was *old* old, but their fifteen-year difference in ages put him in a different demographic.

"I'm just happy," he said.

That first weekend, Luke's wife was away with her book group up in the mountains. Luke made Emily pancakes, which they ate in bed. They made love three times a day and bathed in her claw-foot tub.

For the rest of the month that Stephen was in India, Luke came by every weekday morning with pastries, and he often brought her a plant. At the police department he'd been promoted to detective sergeant, making it easy for him to slip out. On his way to her place, he stopped by C'est Si Bon for coffees to go and croissants packaged in pink boxes. Maybe cops only ate donuts when they were on cop duty. He brought Captain treats and toys, and she was sure the dog looked forward to his visits as much as she did.

Luke set the coffee and pastries on her kitchen table, uncapped a black coffee for her, a coffee with cream for himself, and patted his big lap. She eased onto it, and they sipped and nibbled. If anyone had told Emily she would someday fall for a cop with a tidy haircut who wore polyester pants, she would have said they were out of their mind.

Once when Luke was taking a shower, his pants draped over a chair back, pleats lined up, she looked at his driver's license and wrote down his home address. Then she searched his phone for his wife's phone number, and after he left, Emily called. She needed to hear Connie's voice. It would tell Emily what she was up against. When his wife answered, her voice sounded smaller than Emily expected, and she was infused with hope like a newly watered plant.

Luke said Connie would have to end the marriage, and he had a plan. If they were seen together, news would get back to Connie and she'd kick him out, so Luke took Emily to a cop baseball game, a cop dinner, and a sex offenders' conference for law enforcement officials. His wife only liked going with him to events and conferences if there was a shopping mall nearby. At the conference, someone called him Father McCormick. He had a rare ability to draw confessions from perpetrators.

His cop friends were curious about her. He introduced her as his friend Emily. Why would he have brought her there, or anywhere, if he had no intention of leaving his wife?

"If she doesn't catch us now, she never will," he said.

"You want her to, so she won't," Emily said. "Murphy's Law."

As Emily predicted, no one tattled.

Luke said the last time he went to church Jesus watched him from up on the cross and Luke was sure Jesus thought he was the biggest hypocrite ever, no better than the losers he interviewed.

Cops were supposed to be aggressive, but Luke was as passive as a bowl of chocolate Kisses.

"Geminis," she teased, "you're fine with living two lives, aren't you?" and he had said yes, yes he was. There was his life at home with his family and his life with her.

Stephen returned from India. They resumed their quiet life. But she hadn't cleaned the house well enough.

"Where'd all these plants come from?" he said. "It's a jungle in here."

"The nursery," she said, and focused on the book she was reading, Alan Watts's *The Wisdom of Insecurity.*

Stephen went to shower and when he returned, he was holding Luke's shaving cream can. "Barbasol?" he said, and jiggled the can at her.

That's all it took for her to confess. They sat on the sofa for hours and cried together. Stephen said he'd stay if she agreed to stop seeing the cop. She shook her head.

"I'm in deep," she said.

That night Stephen packed two suitcases and moved out.

The next day, she and Luke had lunch at a neighborhood café, and afterward they stood in the parking lot by his unmarked car. She told him she loved the plants he brought her—a hydrangea, pyracantha, wisteria, narcissus—but they were a poor substitute for him.

"Trust me, my body may be with my wife," he said, and tapped his chest, "but my heart is with you."

"And the check's in the mail." Inside she was crumbling.

He took in the salty air, closed and opened his eyes with what looked like resolve, and said, "I'll leave her. I'll tell her tonight."

"Really?"

"Yes, really."

Luke grew teary-eyed. His green eyes glimmered like marbles. Here was this big cop in a white shirt and tie and pinstriped pants getting all teary-eyed in a parking lot. He pulled her to him, and they hugged. The glaring sun recorded the moment as the wind riffled his hair. As she drove from the parking lot, she looked into her rearview and saw him pull a cloth hankie from his pocket and dab at his eyes.

The man on the beach grew closer. At a distance, he looked so much like Luke. Captain got to his feet and stretched, muscles rippling along his rib cage. If it *was* Luke, what would she say? Captain licked her toes, his signal for a swim.

They ran to the water. The sky was electric, and the day was just this side of hot—a perfect May afternoon. Kids still in school, tourists not yet crowding the beach.

The sand warmed the soles of her feet. She dove into the waves and the cold saltwater pulled her into the moment like a conductor before the first note. She surfaced and treaded water. Captain bobbed toward her.

The day after Luke's parking lot vow, he stopped by with a pink box. She knew something was wrong the moment he stepped into her apartment. He set the box down and sat. His eye twitched and his mouth turned down at the corners.

"What?" she said, standing before him, hugging herself.

"I tried," he said. "I can't."

She sighed.

Luke equivocated. "You're in the fast lane," he said. "You'll get bored with me. Then what will I have? Not you, not a wife, my kids hating me, half my pension."

What could she say to that? It was a possibility. If he did leave his wife and she did grow bored, what would happen then? He was in a different phase of life, but that didn't make this any easier. Missing him made her teeth ache.

In her apartment that last time they were together, he said, "One day I will come back for you. It will be the first of the month. You'll be at our spot. I'll be walking the shoreline. I'll find you."

He could be so romantic and wasn't ashamed of romance, unlike guys her age who were so into themselves they sexted pictures of their most private body part to women they just met.

And here he was now, on the beach, remembering their anniversary, coming for her.

From this distance in the water, under the noonday sun, Luke looked as if he had lost weight. He had said his doctor wanted him to lose twenty-five pounds for the sake of his heart. His hair looked grayer or maybe it was the sun's white-hot glare. Time changed you, no matter how much you paid a plastic surgeon.

Emily and Captain swam to shore. Captain shook, flinging droplets of water like ice crystals.

Luke was only a hundred feet away now, his back to her.

"Hey!" she said. "You came."

He turned and in a thick French accent, said, "*Pardonne-moi?*"

It wasn't Luke but only someone who looked like Luke, his doppelganger, of all things.

"I'm so sorry," she said, backing away. "You look like someone I know."

"I wish I were him." A spray of chest hair popped like a geyser from the V of his tee-shirt.

She escaped across the sand, Captain at her heels. She cut across the beach and fell onto her blanket. In the sickly-sweet blue sky, a jet left a smudgy contrail.

Her eyes burned with tears. How could she have ever imagined Luke would return? Captain nuzzled her. She pulled him close. Luke's lookalike moved away until he was a shimmering stick figure.

Longing for Luke had gone on long enough. If she didn't move on now, she never would. She'd become one of those sad jaded women who hated men but wanted one anyway. This beach town was full of them.

She had to get rid of everything Luke had given her. She gathered all the cards and dog toys in a trash bag and set it outside her door to carry to the dumpster. She loaded the potted plants into the Saab—except for the ficus. It had grown too tall to fit.

She latched Captain into his car crate and entered Luke's address into her GPS.

She took the La Paz exit, made a few turns, and was soon on his street. She held her breath when she reached his home, a nondescript beige house in an even more nondescript housing tract. She let out her breath. It was so ordinary, like the rest of the houses on the block, but there were so many cars parked along the street—strange for the middle of a weekday.

She pulled into the driveway beside his car, a late-model Lexus. That was odd. She hadn't meant to see Luke; she had picked this time of day because he'd be at work.

She threw open the car door and stepped onto the driveway. She let Captain out of his crate and unloaded the plants. The Christmas cactus, oleander, hydrangea, pyracantha, wisteria, narcissus—all of them she set by the front door. Screw Luke and his nice cozy life and everything about him. She was finished. Done. Kaput. Captain trotted about the yard, marking territory.

As she set down the last plant, the front door yawned open. There she was, a woman so petite a strong wind might blow her over, yet she was the hedge in Luke's life, constant and rooted, while Emily was a potted plant, easily knocked over, transient, forgettable.

The woman's eyes were rimmed in red. Luke had said she worked till five. It was just after three.

"So many nice plants," the woman said. "What florist are you with?"

Emily looked for Captain, who was off in the corner of the yard, sniffing.

"People are so kind to send so many beautiful things," the woman said.

"I'm not with a florist."

The wife looked confused. "I'm Connie. It's very nice of you to bring these lovely plants. Luke loved gardening. So tragic, out in the desert . . . looking for succulents, that rattlesnake. You'd think he would have heard it."

Emily was stunned. Wait a minute. Luke died?

"Aren't they supposed to rattle?" Connie said. "What a day to forget his phone."

Emily forced out words. "I'm so sorry for your loss." Emily's voice broke as she called for Captain to return to her side, to rescue her from this awkward, horrible moment. She looked around for somewhere to sit. She felt queasy and was on her way to fainting.

Connie must have seen this because she said, "Why don't you come in, dear?"

Captain trotted over. Emily grabbed a leash from the car, hooked his collar, and tied the leash to the metal outdoor sofa.

Connie took her by the hand and led her inside. The wife's hand was warm and soft. The hand that had last touched Luke, had most likely held his hand, smoothed back his hair.

Inside the foyer, framed family photos lined the walls and stood on the long table beneath them. A crowd of mourners—cops in uniforms with wives, older folks, a few kids—stood around a buffet table and sat on chairs, eating and talking.

Connie introduced her to a few people and to the son. He was Luke at twenty. Eyes sea glass green, hair like Luke's, only darker and a little longer in front and shaved on the sides.

"How'd you know my dad?" he said when Connie wandered off.

"He helped me once with a burglary," Emily said. "Maybe twice." It was so easy to lie once you began, like running downhill.

"Nice to meet you. I better go," Emily said.

She was on her way down the hallway when Connie called after her. "Leaving so soon?"

"I have to get back," Emily said.

"Nice of you to bring the plants," Connie said, walking her outside.

"Thanks for having me." Emily reached out to shake her hand, and Connie strong-armed her into a hug.

Before Connie let go, she said, "Just so you know, you weren't the first."

Emily had never wanted to consider this.

"But you're the one he might have left me for." Connie released her and gave her a sad look.

"And you're the one he could never leave," Emily said. At that moment the wife drifted off to somewhere else, a distant star, wherever Luke was. She nodded at Emily.

"You take care," Connie said, not unkindly, and disappeared into the house.

The front door closed. Emily was about to lock Captain into his car crate when she let him sit on the passenger's seat. She got in and stared at the brown garage door. He leaned over, licked her cheek. She jumped out to retrieve the oleander, set it on the back seat, and pulled into the quiet, car-lined, beige suburban street.

147

CRAZY FOR YOU

When I moved into Levi's apartment in the converted motel on Placentia Avenue, the blue neon "I" of THE PLACENT_A ARMS sign was burned out. I worried it was an omen, a feng shui gaffe. It made me think too damn much of placenta, birthing, and that whole entire mess—not a good thing when the sight of blood makes you faint. I'd grown used to most things and figured I'd grow used to the sign, if I didn't leave Levi or go crazy first. But I hadn't grown used to it, and I was still here. It was going on three months, and my feeling of foreboding had only increased.

The Arms, a chipping aqua U-shaped construction, was clean enough, but Levi's apartment above the fray on the second story, right-hand corner, was growing smaller and duller by the day. So was Westside Costa Mesa, once idyllic cattle grazing land, then an agricultural haven. Now, about the only things that grew wildly were the illegal immigrant population, low-income housing, and gangs. So different from where I was from. If I spoke the language, it might be different, or if I was brunette. But I was blonde, the only *gringa* in our apartment complex.

I pulled a folding chair onto the balcony overlooking the pool, such as it was, and lighted a hand-rolled cigarette, the only tobacco I could afford these days. In the Arms's courtyard just below sat a square swimming pool that had seen better days. Sorry little children with loser parents—why else would they be living at the Placent_a Arms?—splashed in its murky depths. Even the mourning doves that inhabited the adjacent kumquat tree seemed wary of the pool, but then Southern California was mired in a ubiquitous drought, and the pool must've been better than nothing, although you'll make yourself believe pretty much anything if your life depends on it.

At night, after a drink or two, as I watched the lights beneath the water, all blue and tropical, I imagined I was at some lush Orange County resort and was one of the beautiful people. The reverie never lasted long, though, because one drunk resident or another would start singing off-key—Barry Manilow, Aerosmith, pop Latino—reminding me I was *not* in posh Newport Beach, the next city over, or in Laguna Beach, just down the coast, but in lovely Costa Misery. My sister Leonora, a nurse, left home back east to work for a plastic surgeon—the perks included discounted *enhancements*—and I followed when I quit my teaching job, all because of Levi.

Levi was sixteen when we met, seventeen when we started spending time—backstage, on the football field, in cars. I was Levi's drama teacher, thirty-three years old but young-looking for my age. My friends called him jailbait, this sleek pretty boy with seafoam-green eyes and abs to die for. I lusted after the kid, but after my soon-to-be ex-husband caught us in my car in the parking lot outside Bob's Big Boy and threatened to have me fired, I decided I needed my teaching credential more than I needed Levi, resigned, and moved here. I saw what happened to other teachers who crossed the line, who forgot they were teachers and not teenagers.

A year later, when Levi turned eighteen, he quit school and found me. He was of age but still too young for me. I was living with Leonora and her three dogs, substitute teaching in Costa Misery along bus routes; the trip cross-country had killed my beater, and I let my driver's license expire. The better school districts never seemed to have an opening, and I didn't want a full-time gig at just any school. Levi had already rented the furnished apartment at the Arms, and I planned on spending just a few days, thinking this would help to get him out of my system. But he guilt-tripped me into moving in, said he wouldn't even be out here if not for me.

"Mimi, the guy's a loser," Leonora said. "You can do better." But I was addicted to Levi's body, his skin like silk, and I was tired of being one of Leonora's pack.

My stomach growled. I lighted another cigarette and looked at my watch. Five o'clock. Levi would be home soon. I went inside to throw something together for dinner.

Levi worked as a handyman. Twenty bucks an hour, sometimes more. Not what he thought he was worth, but it paid the rent, bought the beer. He told me stories about the rich people's houses where he spent the day—painting the walls of a nursery with designer paint or re-tiling a Jacuzzi. He described how, at one home, the outdoor pool connected with the interior of the house through a man-made cave with faux boulders you had to swim through. *So* Orange County.

Another client owned two houses side by side—one of them the family lived in, while the other one was the kids' playhouse. *Playhouse!* Homeless people lined up at church soup kitchens and lived in parks and alleys around Costa Misery. Life was indeed unfair. And I was a little envious. Some people in Orange County had too much while others had so damn little.

In Westside Costa Misery, where we lived, everyone—the Hispanics, the working-class heroes, even the dogs—were, for the most part, lackluster. Artists lived here, too, and added color, but every day I went online to read the local crime log. So much of the crime in coastal Orange County happened right around where I lived. Here were the factories, auto shops, *taquerias* and *lavandarias*, and so many of us were scraping by, but on the east side, which bordered Newport Beach, that's where the real money was, that's where the Orange County life I'd imagined and fantasized resided. I'd been to Disneyland but never got why they called it the Happiest Place on Earth, not with all those screaming children and tourists with blue-white legs and lunky cameras strangling their necks. But a house on the east side, now that would make for a happy day, every day.

Levi came home from installing shelves in what he said looked like the kitchen of a TV cooking show: *marble*—not granite—countertops, Viking stovetop, a fridge the size of our bathroom. He rambled on about how the homeowner didn't have a wife. I was standing at the stove, stirring Arborio rice, adding vegetable broth every few minutes, to make risotto. What you pay for at a restaurant when you order risotto are not the ingredients, but the time it takes for some sadly underpaid restaurant worker to make the rice swell all plump-like.

Biscuits that I'd rolled out with my marble pastry roller, my most prized kitchen implement, and baked in the dollhouse-sized oven with a stovetop that only had three working burners, cooled on the rack.

Levi could see I was down, so he kissed my cheek hard and wrapped his arms around me from behind. After a day among kids who treat substitute teachers like dog do, Levi's touch was heaven. He snaked his hand beneath my skirt and found my sweet spot. At first I shooed him away—you can't leave risotto for *one minute*—but once Levi got on a certain track, there was no stopping him.

Levi liked to give me pleasure, or maybe he knew this was the main thing he had to offer, so he got on his knees and buried his face down *there*, and I about went nuts but kept stirring until I just couldn't take it anymore. I let the spoon clatter to the counter and dropped to the aqua-and-white linoleum. I pulled Levi down with me. It didn't take us long, which is another thing I liked about Levi—he wasn't one of those guys who needed to linger and stretch it out.

We finished, and I washed my hands before returning to my risotto, but it was too late. The pot of rice was one sticky clod. I dumped it into the sink. Levi cracked two beers and ordered a pizza. While we waited, we went out onto the balcony. We drank our beers and watched the pool where a lone pink inner tube floated.

"Get this, Mimi," he said. "This house I was at today, it also has a three-car garage. Three fucking cars! And there's just one dude who lives there, with his kids."

"Where's the wife?" I said, taking a swig.

He shook his head. "Died from cancer or something—and not long ago. There's fucking art all over the place and expensive dishes are stacked in a monster cabinet the length of our living room wall. His brats have these little motorized cars they drive around the neighborhood. They live on this dead end—a *cul de sac*. Old-money Costa Mesa, looks like. People have got serious funds over there. More than they need."

"Some people have all the luck."

"We deserve that kind of life," he said.

"Everyone thinks they do."

"But we *really* do. His fucking housecleaner knows more about his stuff and what he has than he does. He has so much crap, he wouldn't miss a few things disappearing."

"I hate it when you sound stupid," I said. "You think you can just help yourself? Is that what you're saying?"

Levi shrugged, took a long pull off the bottle, and slipped out of his red leather cowboy boots, setting them inside the doorway. He pulled off his T-shirt. He was still that sleek boy, a beauty. His curly brown hair was streaked blond, and he had just the right amount of growth on his face. His teeth were white-white, and his bare feet were perfect. He could be a model, that's how handsome he was. Feet and teeth, I've always said, need to be superior. His physique made me overlook the fact that he wasn't the brightest bulb in the room.

"Shepard needs a nanny for his kids, pretty much right away," Levi said. "Someone smart enough to tutor. He's running an ad but says he can't find the right person."

"I'm a teacher," I reminded him. "Not a nanny."

"But you *could* be a nanny . . . for a time. Then we'd both be working there."

"You think he's going to go for a fricken handyman and his older girlfriend both working for him? Please."

"Don't call me a handyman," he snapped.

"That's what you are, babe."

He looked hurt. "I aspire to more."

"Sure, you do," I said. "I just don't like where you're headed with this." I stroked his chest and tickled his nipples, which always put him in a good mood.

"Shepard would like you. I told him about you. He seems lonely. I mean, who wouldn't be—your wife up and dies and leaves you with little kids? But once he sees a pretty young thing like you, his day's suddenly gonna seem a lot brighter. Don't you want to brighten up a widower's day?"

"I'm not that young."

"You're the sexiest thing going." He ran his fingers along my collarbone. "We could both be working there."

"And then?"

"Who knows! But you deserve better'n this." His hands described an arc about him, his voice going low. "You think all the rich fucks in this town work for what they have? A lot of them got old money. Inheritances. Bank accounts handed down. Or they have great gigs, businesses that haul ass. We weren't lucky that way. Shit, Shepard has an entire goddamn library! He's old, but he has money."

"Levi, you're scaring me."

"Don't be scared, baby. How about I just introduce you to him?" He put his hands on my shoulders and looked down at me with his seawater eyes. "C'mon, as long as you don't like him *that* way, and why would you—he's not *me*—it could be fun."

"Ripping off your employer . . . fun, huh?"

He shrugged. "Like I said, it'd be better'n this."

We turned our attention back to the pool and that pink inner tube bobbing about, when a pizza boy came waltzing into the courtyard like a waiter holding a tray, that flat box poised atop his fingers.

"We'd need a plan," I said, as the pizza boy looked up, trilled the fingers of his other hand like we were in some Hollywood musical, and headed for the cement stairway.

"Mims, I'm all about planning," Levi said, pulling a twenty from his pocket.

The stinking economy, even here in glorious Orange County, had pushed substitute teaching gigs further and further apart, so the next day, around lunchtime, I was sitting on the balcony, smoking a hand-rolled and scanning the classifieds. A cherry pie cooled on the counter. I had to do something fast to rescue my financial situation. Levi's truck skidded in. He threw a veggie bologna sandwich together—white bread from Trader Joe's, Dijon mustard, and four slices of fake lunchmeat—and said he was taking me with him to Shepard's house, ten minutes away.

I climbed into his truck, a major gas hog that you just about needed a ladder to get into. As we passed Latinas with long black braids that touched their waists who pushed strollers, and homeless guys wearing tattered backpacks, he said, "Um, by the way, Shepard thinks you're my older sister, so just play it cool."

"Excuse me?"

"I decided he wouldn't like the idea of you being my girlfriend."

"Sometimes you fucking make me wonder."

He nodded, keeping his eyes fixed on the road. "I just thought of it. Brilliant, huh?"

"Yeah, right. Incredible genius you got goin' in that head of yours."

But as we crossed over Newport Boulevard, leaving the less than lovely side of town for the lush, moneyed side where tall eucalyptus swayed in the faint ocean breeze, Costa Misery became Piece of Heaven, California, with its cute cottages; palm trees; rosebushes; magenta bougainvillea; and Jaguars, BMVs, and hybrids in the drives.

We pulled into his boss's driveway. A tall, husky guy in khakis and a polo shirt, with short graying hair, futzed in the garage. He was a bit thick in the middle and wore conservative beige shoes.

"You owe me big-time." I pushed open the door as Mr. Orange County Republican approached us.

"That a promise?" Levi said as I jumped from the cab.

The guy had been a hottie once and was handsome in an almost-fifty way, but he was *so* not my type. He held out his hand. "You must be Levi's sister," he said, giving me a warm handshake. "He didn't tell me you were so pretty."

"He's been forgetting to take his gingko biloba." I played it off, but I was charmed. And it took a lot to charm me.

Levi laughed as if I were the funniest older sister in the entire universe.

"You two get acquainted," said Levi. "The back fence is calling me."

Shepard gave him a thumbs-up and said, "Shall we go inside?" Shepard's eyes were friendly as he gestured me in and hit the electric garage door button. "The kids are at school, but I'll show you around so you can see where you'd be spending your days."

I forced a smile, tried to look interested.

"School's out tomorrow," he said. "I need someone who can be a nanny *and* a teacher. Only occasional sleepovers, when I'm out of town." He had a gap between his front teeth, which were white and even. My first big boyfriend had a gap I would tongue.

"Your brother says you're a teacher."

Brother? Then I remembered.

"I was, back east," I said. "Taught drama and English. I've been substitute-teaching since I moved here. Not a lot of work these days for teachers without seniority."

"That's too bad." He touched my shoulder to direct me into the living room. He must have noticed how my gaze fell on the baby grand because he said, "You play?"

"Used to," I said.

"Like riding a bicycle, don't you think? You're welcome to . . ." He nodded toward it.

"Ah, no. Maybe another time." Being able to play piano impressed people, but it didn't impress me. You could learn anything, if you wanted to.

"Your brother said you like to bake."

"I'm obsessed with making pies." When we have extra money, I almost added.

"You're welcome to bake here, anytime. I can't remember the last time a pie came out of that oven. Just give me a list; I'll buy you what you need."

If it were possible to fall in love with a house, I was falling—hard—especially for the kitchen. With a kitchen like this, I could bake a million pies and never grow bored.

"Like something? Coffee? A soda?" He stuck a glass into the opening of the fridge's front panel and pushed a button. Ice chinked into the glass.

"Diet Coke?"

"Sure thing."

"No glass," I said, so he tore a paper towel from the roll and wiped the top of the can clean before handing it to me. No one had ever done that before, and I swear, he looked different after that. Charming.

We talked about my background and his needs, and an hour later, when the kids were dropped off, he gave them big bear hugs and introduced us.

"Bella and Dante, this is Mimi. She might be helping us out. Want to show her your rooms?" The kids appraised me like I was a new piece of furniture, and then Bella took my hand.

"My room first," she said. Her little brother led the way, running his Hot Wheels police car along the wall.

They showed me their rooms, and I liked them. Levi stuck in his head and said he had to run off for a while, and when he returned at five, he seemed strangely hyper and rushed me to go.

As we pulled away from the curb and headed down the tree-lined street, Levi said, "He's not bad, right?"

"He was fine." I almost added, *he was more than fine.* "But you're low-down." I had never felt so cold toward Levi, not that he noticed.

"He tell you what he does for a living? I think he's a developer or something."

"Something like that," I said.

"Major bucks," he said.

"Construction's taking a dive."

"He say that? Don't believe it." He turned onto a street with high walls hiding homes, pulled over, and put the truck in park. He scooched over, took me in his arms, and started kissing my neck. Melted me every time. Stupid guys who were cute made the best lovers. It was the truly smart ones you had to watch out for, who could skewer your heart with one word.

"C'mon, baby, don't be mad. It's a way for us to get ahead."

"His kids aren't brats," I said. "They're sweet."

He pulled a blanket from under the seat, covered us as he pushed me down with kisses, and said, "After this, we'll go eat. I'm starving."

We sat across from each other at Wahoo's Fish Tacos, a popular haunt on Placentia, down the street from where we lived. The exterior was covered with chipping teal paint. Surf stickers smattered the windows. The menu offered Mexican entrees that weren't gourmet but were good enough, priced for artists and people on limited incomes, and for rich Orange Countians who liked a deal. As he talked about what we'd do with the money—a new truck for him, a kitchen for me—you'd think I was one hungry fish, the way I went for it. I must have been beyond bored. We'd go slow and easy, figure things out, and when we had all the pieces, we'd make our play, he said, but I had a bad feeling.

Levi began staying up late, figuring out where we'd escape to once we had a few of Shepard's more high-end belongings that he would give to a friend of a friend who would split the proceeds. I did a bit of research and learned that Shepard had paintings and antiques worth thousands. He had one Chagall lithograph, *Artist with a Goat, #1026*, that was worth thirty grand. Even inane simple drawings of dolphins that lined the hallway by that overrated Laguna Beach artist, Wyland, sold for three grand apiece. Levi's idea was we'd leave Costa Misery for Mexico. No one can find you down there, he said.

A week into my new nannyhood, as Levi and I were wrapping it up for the day, and I was saying goodbye to the children, Shepard said, "The kids are going to their aunt's. Why don't I take you out to dinner, my thanks for coming to our rescue?"

Levi didn't miss a beat. "Go ahead, sis," he said. "It'd be fun for you."

Sis?

I scanned what I was wearing—jeans, a purple pullover, low-top red Converse. "I'm not exactly dressed up," I said.

"You'd look gorgeous in a flour sack," said Shepard.

Levi winked at me. I shrugged. "Okay, then."

Levi hurried off a little too quickly with a nonchalant wave.

"Let's have a taste before we go," said Shepard. "Pick anything you like from the wine cellar, and I'll meet you out by the pool."

A converted closet off the kitchen with a slate floor and thermostat that said fifty-three degrees served as the cellar. I chose a 1987 Tondonia because I liked the name. He carried our glasses to the back patio beside the pool that was a million times better than the Arms's pool.

"I could get used to this," I said, after we clinked glasses.

"I hope you do." His voice was all syrupy and warm, like the wine.

Soon Shepard and I were in his Jag cruising up Newport Boulevard to Havana, a Cuban restaurant in a funky open-air mall with an oil drum waterfall and tattooed, pierced hipsters. Havana was dark, lit only with candles. You could barely see who was sitting next to you, but the waiter could see well enough to recognize Shepard and make a big deal. It was different being with someone before whom people groveled.

Shepard ordered a bottle of Barolo red. He said it was the king of wines. We toasted and he said to order whatever tickled my fancy. Those were his words. During dinner a second bottle of wine arrived, and for dessert we shared a Cuban flan. Our fingers brushed against one another.

"We're delighted you came to us," he said. "The children like you very much."

"They're sweethearts," I said.

"To be honest, I'm the happiest." He stroked my arm and focused on it as if it were a great treasure. "You've got great skin."

"This light would make anyone look good." I felt guilty over how much I enjoyed his attention. Then I thought, *What the hell. Levi got me into this*, and I gave in. Right then and there I felt myself loosen and open to Shepard. When Shepard's hand found mine, I let it. And when he brought my hand to his lips, I let him. We left the restaurant and returned to his Jag, his arm laced around my shoulder. He opened the passenger's door, and I slid onto the butter-soft leather seats that reclined at the touch of a button. He got in and buzzed down the windows. He turned to kiss me, and I kissed him back, tongued that gap in his front teeth. The wine was talking. His hand found its way under my pullover and then he was in my jeans. I pressed against his fingers and before long, I shuddered. Who cared if he was a conservative and a bit too husky—he had the touch of an angel and was sweet and considerate. He was different from anyone I'd ever been with. Maybe older guys with money could afford to be patient, considerate.

"What about you?" I said into his neck, rubbing him down there.

"There's time for that." He gently removed my hand and kissed it.

When I got home, Levi wanted to know where we went and what we did. He wasn't so laid back anymore. I didn't tell him everything but distracted him with sex. It always worked. I had to keep my OC Republican a secret for now.

But things had changed, and Levi knew it. Now when we arrived at Shepard's in the morning, there was no mistaking the glimmer in Shepard's eyes. He hung around the house to have coffee with me before taking off. On occasion, when everyone was out of the house, we fooled around.

"The dude fucking likes you," Levi said a week later, his eyes flashing. We were in his truck, at a stop light.

"What are you talking about?"

"He's been asking me all about you. He's in love with you."

"He can't be," I said, secretly wishing it were so.

"Hey, it could be good for us." He scowled.

"What do you mean?"

"Shit, what could be better for us than if he wanted to marry you?"

"Excuse me?"

"It wouldn't have to change things between us. No one's as great for you as I am. You'd never go for someone that old. And if you did, I'd kill you." He laughed. "You'd just have to live with him for a time. It would help us pull off our plan."

"You're talking too crazy for me," I said, as we crossed over Newport Boulevard and Piece of Heaven turned back into Costa Misery, with its pawnshops, its dive bars. But that night, after Levi went back out to do who knows what—he wouldn't say—I stood on the balcony and smoked a hand-rolled. As the lighted murky water below pulled my focus, the sounds of the compound drew close—TV, a neighbor singing off-key, kids screaming—and my own version of the lyrics from an old Animals song spun an endless loop in my brain: *I gotta get outta this place, if it's the last thing I ever do.*

The next day after Shepard's sister picked up his kids for an overnight, he said, "Let me take you to the fair. You've been to the Orange County Fair, right?"

"Um, no," I said. I'd left Bumfuck where "hooptedoodle" was a favorite expression, and I had no desire to return.

"Then you got to let me take you," he said.

"Fairs are a Republican thing."

"Pshaw!" He tucked in his turquoise polo shirt with a tiny alligator over the left breast.

"Shouldn't you take your kids?"

"They've been, and I'll take them again before the fair ends," he said. "Tonight, it will be just you and me. How about it?"

I said yes. I said yes to everything—to Levi and his schemes, now to Shepard.

Levi called from another job while I was in the bathroom freshening up; Shepard had run out of work for him. I said I had to work late. I spent more and more time at Shepard's and less and less time at our sorry excuse for a home. It was getting to Levi. I knew because when he talked about Shepard, he no longer used his name but called him motherfucker. "The motherfucker tell you anything interesting?" or "What's up with the motherfucker?" I found a bindle with white powder in Levi's things. His skin was becoming all mottled and he was losing weight. He denied using meth, said he picked it up for a friend, but he was short-tempered and negative. I wanted to escape with Shepard, go someplace where Levi couldn't find me.

Shepard and I walked hand in hand to his dusty blue Jag and moments later were gliding down Broadway to Newport and up to Del Mar, his hand on my knee, my hand on his thigh, to where the dark sky was lit up all red from the rides and the midway. The Ferris wheel spun lazily around, its colorful, happy life temporary—like mine, I feared. This happiness wouldn't last—it couldn't; it hadn't been a part of the plan for me to fall for an Orange County Republican. Levi would never let me have Shepard. I wanted to confess and tell Shepard what Levi was planning, but I didn't know how I could put it where he wouldn't just fire me and tell me to be on my way.

We parked and walked toward the lights, toward the Tilt-A-Whirl and the roller coaster with purple neon cutting the black sky, teenagers on all sides of us running amok, clutching cheap stuffed animals and stalks of cotton candy. Shepard bought us caramel apples, fried Twinkies, and roasted corn on the cob. We got wristbands and drank draft beer from big red cups.

It was going on eleven and the fairgoers poured through the gates, probably to get a jump on the freeways. Shepard and I moved against the flow, heading toward the livestock area, past Hercules the giant horse, llama stalls, and the corral where they held pig races.

My phone rang—Levi's ringtone—but I ignored it, and I feared it. Levi said he could always find me. Something about the GPS setting on my phone and how he rigged it. Cell phones didn't make you freer—they made your whereabouts known, and I didn't like it one bit, this hold Levi had on me.

Couples lingered in the shadows. Shadows scared me. I worried Levi might be hiding in them. Lately everything got on his nerves, and he suspected everyone. He'd screamed at the next-door neighbor to quit his fool singing. He even pierced the pink inner tube in the pool because he no longer liked seeing it floating there.

Shepard directed me to the metal bleachers around the cattle arena. He picked me up, set me on one so our faces were level, and kissed me. "You make me so happy," he said.

This tall, bulky man had grown on me. He pulled a little robin's-egg-blue box from his pocket and flipped it open. A diamond solitaire.

He took the ring from the box and slid the ring on my finger. "You will, won't you?" he said. "Marry me?"

Levi was leaning over the railing of the balcony, smoking with one of his low-life loser buddies, when I arrived home at midnight. I'd taken off the ring and sequestered it at the bottom of my tampon holder.

The light from the water bounced off Levi and his buddy, whose name I forgot. I gave them a half-hearted wave. Levi smiled his lizard-cold smile.

"Where've you been?" He flicked the cigarette butt down into the pool as his buddy took off.

"Had to stay with the kids until Shepard got home." I took a cigarette from Levi's pack on the cement floor.

"Fuck you did," he said.

I gave him a long look. It was always better to say less than more.

"Where's the ring?" he said.

"What ring?"

"This'll only work if you're straight with me about the motherfucker."

I started for the apartment, when he grabbed my arm. "I'm gonna tell him all about you. You weren't supposed to fall in love with the asshole. You love me, remember?"

I wrenched my arm away and hurried inside. I poured a glass of water, trying to think.

Levi hurried in behind me. "Don't fucking walk away from me, Mimi."

"I'll do what I want."

"Fuck you will." He pulled me to him, pressed his mouth against mine, hiked his hand up my top. "C'mon, baby. What happened to us?"

I pulled free. "Leave me alone, you asshole," I said.

"I own you. I came all the way out here to find you and claim you and now you're mine."

"Whatever drug you're doing, it's making you crazy," I said.

"Crazy for you." He grabbed me with one hand and undid his belt buckle with the other.

I'd never given in to a man forcing me, and I wasn't about to now. I tried pushing Levi away, but his grasp on my arm only grew tighter.

"You always liked it with me before," he said. "Mr. O.C. motherfucker better'n me now?" His face looked strained, a Halloween mask. "He won't want you when I tell him who you really are, when I tell him everything you planned. He'll take his ring back and then where will you be?"

"What *I* planned?"

He jammed his hand down my pants and hurt me and that's when something snapped. My prized marble roller sat on the counter behind me, where it always was. I felt for it with my free hand and almost had it, but it slipped away. My hand alighted on Levi's hammer. I brought it around and cracked it against Levi's skull as hard as I could. His seafoam-green eyes went wide, as if he were seeing me for the first time. Then he crumpled to the linoleum. A trickle of blood issued from his ear.

"Levi!" I said. "Shit!"

The way his eyes gazed into the living room without blinking gave him a peaceful look I had never seen.

I tried to think. Should I pack up my things, including my pastry roller, and split? I considered cleaning my fingerprints off everything in the apartment, but I wouldn't be able to get rid of every little hair, every little cell of mine that had flaked off. I knew about DNA.

I could be easily tied to Levi, even without a car or California driver's license, without my name on the month-to-month lease or on bills. I talked to Levi on my cell phone all the time. I could also be tied to Levi through Shepard. They would visit Levi's former employer and find me there, loving my new life.

No, I couldn't leave.

I pulled down the shades and locked the door. I wiped my fingerprints off the hammer and put Levi's hand, still warm, around the handle. I turned on the shower as hot as I could stand, peeled off my clothes, and stepped in. It would calm me and help me think. As the scalding water poured down my face, it came to me, what I would say and do: *I came home, Levi was here with a drug-dealing buddy, I took a shower and heard something, and when I got out of the shower, I found my boyfriend on the floor.*

I turned off the water, wrapped myself in a towel, and jumped into my role. I hurried out to the kitchen as if I'd heard something bad, and found Levi hurt on the kitchen floor. I bent down to see what was wrong. Water puddled about me and mixed with Levi's blood. I ran screaming from the apartment onto the balcony. As I started down the steps, the towel slipped from my body, and I let it. I was a crazy naked lady. Residents, men in underwear and T-shirts and women in nightgowns, emerged from their hovels.

"Call the police!" I made a good hysteric. Someone had done in my poor boyfriend.

Women called in Spanish to each other. More than once I heard the word "loco." A short, dark woman with gold front teeth wrapped me in a Mexican blanket, patted my wet hair, and cooed to me in Spanish. The sirens grew close. A crowd had gathered around us and upstairs at the doorway to the apartment.

There would be an investigation, but after a while I would be cleared. No one ever saw us fight. There was no insurance settlement coming. Why would I kill my boyfriend? The authorities would search instead for the lowlife who did him—or not. Probably not. Who cared about one more druggie dude going bye-bye? The first chance I got I would call Shepard, tell him details about what happened that he might have heard about on the news. I would tell him how Levi made me say I was his sister, had threatened my life, even, but had never wanted me to fall for Shepard. I would remind Shepard that I loved him, every inch of him. Shepard believed in me, would never think I could do something like this.

I knew how to be patient. Shepard and Piece-of-Heaven, California, would eventually be mine, and before long, the ring would be back on my finger.

DOORS

Grace's alarm went off at 7:00 a.m. instead of 7:30 because her boyfriend, Freddie, didn't own an alarm clock or a smart phone, and if he was late for work and got fired, it would be her fault. He said this was a girlfriend's job. On the one hand, she was annoyed. On the other, it felt good to be needed. She used to do that for her mom, too, when she was alive. Her mother swore she couldn't hear the alarm and made Grace wake her.

Grace was in the eleventh grade, and the first-period bell rang at 8:30. Breakfast was Pop-Tarts and chocolate milk. When her mother died a year ago, her dad lost his sales job because he was rude to a customer. Now he spent his days in front of the TV, where he sat now, with his cup of black coffee and dry toast. She kissed his cheek before she left for school and he said, "Study hard, girl. You can be anything you want to be."

He wasn't the best example.

She said, "I'm worried about you."

He put the TV on mute and patted the sofa. "Don't be worried."

"Since Mom died, you haven't been the same."

"Wouldn't you think it strange if I *was* the same?"

"I guess," she said, "but I miss the old you."

"I miss the old me, too. But you're sixteen. Many years from now you'll understand."

"I gotta go," she said. He gave her a sad smile and unmuted the TV.

At first her old Toyota Corolla didn't want to start. "Dammit," she said, and pumped the gas pedal, maybe too hard. Freddie said she shouldn't be so impatient with the car, that the engine flooded easily. Well, Freddie could just wake himself up. But then the car started, and she drove away from their tract of three-bedroom ranch homes where all the streets had presidential names—McKinley, Madison, Hamilton.

Fifteen minutes later, she arrived at Freddie's apartment in a neighborhood that had seen better days. Her dad called where he lived the wrong side of the tracks. An apartment house with bars on the first-floor windows. What kind of respectable place was that, certainly not the sort of place a good boy lived. But Freddie wasn't a boy. He was eighteen, and in certain cultures, eighteen was old.

She parked, climbed the outdoor stairway, and let herself in with her key. The apartment smelled of old beer and trash that needed to be carried to the dumpster. She threw open the front window. In his bedroom, Freddie splayed across the bed, the blond hair on his legs lit up from the sun.

"Freddie! Time to get up."

He didn't stir.

"Yoohoo, Freddie!"

She gave his bare shoulder a shake. He felt clammy to the touch, as if he'd been out running.

He groaned.

"You have to go to work, and I have to get to school."

"Five more minutes," he grumbled.

In the kitchen she filled a pan with water for coffee. While she waited for it to boil, she gazed out the window at the swimming pool below, where a lone pink Styrofoam noodle floated on the surface.

A body shop sat across the street from the apartment. The sound of a car rising on a hydraulic lift reached her. She never before had a boyfriend who quit school. He dropped out in his senior year before she met him. School took too long, he said. He needed money now, and there was good money in detailing.

She returned to the bedroom with the coffee and shook his shoulder. "Up, you." She set the mug on his nightstand, which he'd found on the street and hauled upstairs.

He reached for her hand. "Come to bed," he said.

"Noooooo," she said. "I gotta go."

He propped himself up on his elbows and squinted at her. His blue eyes caught the light like the crystal goblets her mother once used to set the table for Sunday dinner. He reached into the drawer of his nightstand and retrieved a brown vial. He tapped a crooked white line onto a geode slab and used a straw with red stripes to snort it.

"Wooeee," he said, shaking his head. "You want some?"

Grace deliberated. "I'm gonna be late if I don't leave now."

"Meet you back here after school, then?"

As she descended the outdoor stairway, in her head she heard an old song her father liked, something about having to get out of this place, if it was the last thing you ever do.

After algebra, second-year Spanish, and AP English, Grace returned to Freddie's empty apartment. She dropped her books on the old lumpy sofa he'd also found on the street. She found a cigarette butt in the ashtray, lit it, and took out her homework. Her algebra grade bobbed around a C, yet in Spanish, *muy bueno*, she got straight A's.

She opened her textbook and translated Spanish into English.

Yes, sir, I like to eat mangoes. No, Mrs. Lopez, I do not drink milk.

There was a loud bang across the street at the auto-repair shop. She ran to the window. Across the street a gaggle of men in blue jumpsuits gathered around a car. Had it fallen off the lift?

Grace sat back down with her textbook and breezed through Spanish, then started on geography homework. A newspaper clipping fluttered out. She plucked it from the air.

Morocco is famous for its spices, bazaars, and decorative tile. You can safely travel to Morocco if you don't flaunt being an American.

Was anywhere safe for Americans? Was anywhere safe for her? Even this suburban Orange County beach city did not feel safe. Last year her English teacher had them write from the perspective of five years out. Her story was all about the fun things she'd done, the trip to France her mother was going to take her on, her fantasy wedding in the mountains by Lake Arrowhead. Those dreams were in the toilet now.

She lit another half-smoked cigarette and blew a perfect smoke ring before she let the smoke drift from her nose.

Freddie busted through the door, said, "Hey, babe!" and beelined for the refrigerator. "Talk about a day!" He popped the cap off a bottle of beer. "You want one?"

"I hate beer," she said, closing the book.

He stood in the doorway to the kitchen. "I have something you'll like." He flopped into the big chair, the stuffing squeezed out one arm. He sucked on the bottle. She closed her book.

"A surprise." He sat up and dug into his pocket.

She perked up. Surprises were one of the remaining joys of being alive. Because her mom died, they didn't even get a Christmas tree. Her gift was a gift card to Walmart.

He unfolded a tiny packet. Little squares of paper with red dots in the center.

"What is it?" She sat on the arm of the chair and peered at the specks.

"Acid." He held them out to her. "Have one."

Her dad had told her about the sixties and Woodstock, and had shown her the movie, but she had never done LSD.

He set a tiny square on the tip of his tongue and curled it into his mouth like a lizard.

"What'll happen?" she said.

He swept his arm through the air and smiled like a carnie. "It'll make this shithole look like a palace."

In the palm of her hand, the teensy square of paper reminded her of those thin paper strips with red dots she had as a kid that you pounded with a hammer to make a gunshot sound. She placed the square on her tongue.

"Fasten your seat belt, little girl." He patted his lap.

She used to sit on her father's lap. It was the only time she felt close to him. But he'd grown thin and sad and no longer encouraged her to come that close.

She slid from the arm of the chair onto Freddie's lap.

"What'd you do in school today?" He drank from the bottle and tipped it her way. "Sure you don't want some?"

She sipped and made a face. The liquid felt like static as it negotiated the throughway of her throat. Freddie's blond curls glistened, and his smile turned devilish, but his blue eyes were like sharp ice she might fall through.

She told him about her day and asked about his, and he went on and on about the rich people's cars he fixed and how one had the console filled with change he helped himself to, that and gift cards to Target. He pulled one from his pocket and handed it to her.

"For you, my princess."

The circles on the card were so red. "You could get fired," she said.

"They'll never miss it," he said.

She cued up music on her phone. An old song her dad liked but her friends made fun of. The Eagles, "Peaceful Easy Feeling." She got to her feet and swayed. Then a faster song, then another, that the two of them danced to.

"Yeah, baby," he said, his eyes closed. "You should be a dancer."

She went to the window. Outside the sky had turned violet and the chain-link fence that separated the apartment complex from the property next door was now pink and baby blue. The factory looked like a playground.

"You coming onto it yet?" he said in that sleepy voice that had made her like him.

"My grandpa lost his false teeth in the toilet once," she said. "It's a good thing he forgot to flush. I found them."

"You got a funny family," he said.

Taylor Swift came on. Freddie always made fun of her but now he sang along and sounded like a frog. She turned around to tell him so, but he looked a little bit like a wolf.

"I don't feel so good." She pressed her face against the cool window.

Outside the sky flashed neon blue, like that bar sign out on Newport Boulevard.

"Dial it down," she said to the sky.

"What?" Freddie was back in his chair, lying back, arms behind his head.

"The sky. It's too bright," she said. "Do you like the door?"

In the wood grain of Freddie's front door were whorls, like a thumbprint, and they swirled about like the beginning of her dad's favorite Hitchcock movie. She wanted to be home now, watching a movie with him.

He ambled over to the door as she ran her hand across it.

"It's so beautiful," she said.

"It's just a door," he said, unimpressed.

He could shut her down with just a few words. He turned on the TV to the five o'clock news. Reports of bad things in the White House—what else was new?

"Turn it off," she said.

He kept watching. He looked even more like a wolf now, with that pointy chin and ears.

She threw open the door, ran down the stairs to the edge of the parking lot, and watched cars pass.

She heard him behind her, footfalls that sounded like cymbals.

"What're you doing? Don't be crazy, now." He pulled her back.

The workers across the street were staring, and she was sure she could hear them mumbling to themselves. Her head felt like a dollhouse without the roof. They knew what she was thinking and agreed that she was one screwed-up girl who would never amount to anything.

A car headed her way, moving as slow as the Karo syrup they used when her mother made them pancakes. Grace almost wanted to jump into the street, but she needed a fast car, something that would plow her down without hurting too much.

Freddie pulled her into the lot, past the pool, and back upstairs.

"Hey, I'm sorry," he said. "It's a beautiful door. I love the door."

The chain-link had turned a brighter shade of pink and blue. There was a jumble of sounds: bees buzzing, metallic scrapes, and hysterical laughter coming from the apartments. Her heart pounded like a steel drum.

He wore a shit-eating grin as he held a sweating beer bottle to her mouth. "Drink it," he said. "It'll help."

She couldn't drink it but held it against her face. The cold reminded her of when she was eight years old, sledding with her cousins down the hill by their cabin in the mountains by the lake. She'd been happy then. Everyone had been—her mother, father, the relatives.

"It's so late," she said. "I gotta go home."

"Girl, you can't drive now. Relax. You hungry? I'll make us something. Nachos? You want nachos?"

He guided her into the kitchen and sat her down. He poured a bag of chips onto a dish, found a jar of cheese sauce in the cabinet, dumped it onto the chips, and slid the entire enterprise into the microwave. Two minutes later, he withdrew a steaming, smoking mass of bubbling goo.

This was her life now, waking Freddie for work, eating bad food for dinner, no one missing her.

With a pair of tongs, Freddie dropped nachos on plates. He slid a plate her way, opened two beers and set one before her.

"This is the life, in'n it?" He couldn't stop laughing.

She bit into a chip. The slimy orange sauce felt like axle grease in her mouth. *Oh yeah, this is the life, all right.* Life with Freddie would be a lifetime of bad meals that he thought were good.

Grace dumped her plate into the sink.

"What'd you do that for?" Freddie said.

"Don't you want more?"

He stopped chewing. "More than what?"

"More than furniture you find on the street, more than stupid nachos with fake sauce, just more. I want to go to college. I don't want a stupid job taking care of rich people's anything, stealing from them."

"You're not being very nice," he said. His mouth turned down at the edges.

Grace poured a glass of water, looked out the window at the auto shop. It was no longer pink and blue but gray and dark purple. It would never be better than this. Her head was going to explode.

Freddie chewed so loud he sounded like he was sifting through gravel. A smear of cheese sauce dirtied Freddie's T-shirt like a wound.

She stuffed her books into her backpack and turned the knob of the door that earlier had looked sublime. Now it was just a door with ugly wood paneling. The whorls were frowning at her. She opened it and walked outside.

He called after her. "Where're you going? Get back here!" His voice echoed off the u-shaped walls of the converted motel.

She moved deliberately, as if she were hiking down a rock face instead of an outdoor stairway. The steps felt squishy on the soles of her shoes. Above, the periwinkle sky vibrated, a living painting exploding with bursts of color.

Her car sat a football field's length away. She glided past the pool that looked bottomless and scary, made it to the Corolla but passed it, and kept walking. She wouldn't reach her home until past dark and by then she would be on her way to being someone else.

HUNTING SEASON

There was an upside to the misfortune. You could see the stars again. I never realized the sky was so *full* of stars. Before the demise, before the cost of electricity had multiplied, the sky contained so much ambient light from streetlights, store lights, and headlights, it was easy to imagine the stars had abandoned us just as the digital gods had. Seeing the stars gave me hope, and some days, hope was all I had.

Since the demise, the morning sun seemed to shine brighter—too bright. I took my coffee onto the landing. I used to bring my typewriter, a beat-up Olivetti 22, outside to write in the early morning, but last year a law was passed here in California making it illegal to possess a typewriter without a special permit, like weed used to be before it was legalized. Permits were expensive and hard to qualify for. You could get thrown in jail if you were caught with a typewriter and no permit. If ratting on people was your thing, you could rationalize turning someone in because of the monetary reward. I didn't think I knew anyone like that. I hope I didn't.

My second bedroom had a baker's rack lined with typewriters I found here and there and sold to needy writers for a pittance. They learned about my typewriters through trusted friends, or I'd hear about a writer who had no tools, and if they had no money, I gifted them. Only my boyfriend, Wade, knew about my cache.

I lit a hand-rolled cigarette and took a long, mind-numbing puff. My apartment sat on the second floor of the Hideout, a former motel built in the fifties that used to be lemon yellow but had faded to a dingy olive. From my vantage point, I had a view of all the apartments. Just below was the square swimming pool where we once swam, but it was now a swamp, a delight to the family of frogs that had taken up residence and the dragonflies that darted about like reconnaissance pilots. Once, all ten apartments were full, with a waiting list. We had a pool cleaner then, but now with only six apartments occupied, the manager, Miguel, said there was no money for pool cleaning and that I should enjoy it as a pond.

Yet I liked it here. If you were an artist or immigrant, it could do quite nicely. This west side of Costa Mesa, which everyone called Costa Misery, was once an agricultural haven known for its soybean production, but now the only things that grew like weeds were poverty and your worries things might only get worse.

No one ever thought the internet would go down permanently, but it was going on a year now. The government said we should prepare for the long haul. Officials blamed it on Russia. My boyfriend, Wade, said the internet would be down forever and believed it wasn't Russia but our own government that had turned it off as one way to shut up us journalists. I scoffed at his proclamations, yet I feared he might be right. Most of the magazines that remained were government-approved, as were newspapers now as thin as Chinese menus. Before the demise, I made a good living writing about the digital universe for a national magazine. When that ended, I started on my savings. The money was almost gone. That was one thing I appreciated about Wade: he had a steady job driving for UPS, he was stable and kind, and after all my loser boyfriends, I appreciated stability and goodness.

I went back inside and closed the door and curtains. My teal Olivetti sat on the kitchen table. I ran my hand over its hood as if it were a child's forehead. The platen no longer turned so easily, and the keys occasionally skipped, but I loved it. The machine was moody, and Wade said it was because it was Italian, and cute, like me. I didn't like it when he said that. What grown woman likes to be called cute?

I heard boots on the back stairway. I threw a towel over my Olivetti and opened the door. Wade, still in his brown UPS uniform, tromped into the apartment. There was a stiffness to his demeanor, and it worried me. I handed him a beer. We clinked bottles.

"We're getting together tonight at Max's," he said, and scowled a little.

"Who's we?"

"Writers. You know some of them."

Wade didn't like Max. I'd introduced them. When I wrote for *Cloud Wired*, I often used Google staff as sources for articles, which was how I met Max.

"We're getting together to talk about doing an underground paper to get the truth out about what's happening. I'm so tired hearing about Russia." His face grew red. "We need to do something. I don't know how you feel about this, but I hope you'll let us use your typewriters."

"How many?" Give up my typewriters? It was a good cause, but all of them?

"A dozen people said they're in."

"We could be arrested."

Wade gave me a look that said, *You wuss.*

"Anybody could be at the meeting," I said. "Have you vetted everyone? Is it safe?"

"We can't suspect everyone. If people say they want to help, I have to believe they want to help."

"That's a little naïve."

"Look, you don't have to come. I just thought—"

"Of course I'll come." I liked Max even though he could overdo the charm. He does have his good points. When I told him Wade's fledgling group needed a place to meet, he offered his house. But it didn't make Wade like him. Wade distrusted charming dudes as much as, or more than, I did. Still, it was a place to meet, and he appreciated him for that.

The beer calmed my rattled nerves. A plane sputtered across the sky. You hardly ever heard private planes anymore. Airplane fuel was ten times more expensive than gasoline, hardly affordable on shrinking incomes.

Wade had never seemed so worried and preoccupied. He used to wake up happy , even with a hangover. Always so upbeat and optimistic. It once got on my nerves. I wished he were his old bubbly self again.

I set down my beer. "Take off your shirt and turn around." I nudged his shoulder.

He pressed his chest to the straight-backed chair. I worked my fingers down his vertebrae.

"That feels good." He let out a sigh.

My fingers continued walking around to the front of his brown UPS shorts and strayed in a southerly direction. Soon we were splayed out on the sofa, and for a moment I forgot about our personal and worldly woes.

As Wade's Jeep motored down 19th Street on our way to Max's, the tall, darkened streetlamps looked like bored giants with nothing to do. The city no longer wanted the expense of paying for electricity. It was as if the city had given up, decided it didn't need new residents and didn't care about pleasing the current ones.

We passed gaggles of bicyclists, little lights blinking on their handlebars and behind seats. At the crosswalks, you'd think you were in New York City, what with all the pedestrians. The demise sent gasoline prices into the ether, and Southern Californians' cars were no longer living rooms on wheels. Three quarters of the gas stations had closed, and the few that were open saw lines of cars at all hours. Wade gassed up his Jeep at the UPS headquarters and drove as much as he wished.

Max's home sat on the east side of Costa Mesa. The area used to be known as Piece of Heaven because some of the lots were as big as small parks, and the houses were large. On my side of town, the air quality and noise pollution were a hundred times better than when all the body shops, repair shops, and factories spewed chemicals and noise into the air, but it would never be Piece of Heaven, not with the low-income housing and iron bars lining windows and doors. In Piece of Heaven there were no bars over windows.

We turned onto Orange Street. "Remember that guy, Jarred, who started that pirate radio station?" Wade's tone sounded foreboding. I hated that tone.

"Please, not more bad news. What about him?"

"He was arrested."

"For what?"

"His show. You can go to jail for having anything to do with radio. Soon they'll throw you in jail for breathing."

"Who turned him in?"

Wade shrugged. "He used to work at Google. I tried getting the info from Max, but he doesn't know anything."

"What's this world coming to?"

"We're screwed," he said. "That's what it's coming to."

Jarred was gone, with no information on what happened. My online friends from Twitter, Facebook, and Instagram were gone too. All those people I'd never met but felt close to—how would we ever find each other again? Maybe when the internet returned, though Wade thought it never would, not in our lifetimes.

We pulled into the driveway beside Max's old, battered Volvo. In the living room, the setting sun bled orange through the drawn curtains. A half dozen men and two women drank beer and quaffed wine. Max handed me a bottle of Heineken. Before the demise, Max used to be a clean-shaven, groomed fellow who organized and sold metadata to advertising and marketing companies. Now he wore a beard and a navy beanie no matter the weather and grew herbs in his backyard.

He directed me into the kitchen as my boyfriend was subsumed into the group in the living room.

We clinked bottles.

"How's the world treating you, Zoe?" he said.

"It's complicated," I said.

Through the doorway I watched as one of the women in the living room removed several blankets, revealing a vintage 4 bank Underwood typewriter. A chorus of *ooh*s and *ah*s.

"Complicated how?" Max said.

"I've been pondering whether life is simpler when you're just trying to survive, or am I missing sitting on my ass staring at my laptop?"

"You used to complain about how the internet was a huge time suck," he said. "You always gave me a hard time for what I did for a living."

"Good memory," I said.

We tipped our bottles toward each other and took another pull.

"My old buddies would think I was insane to hear me say I like growing herbs," he said.

He riffled through the cabinet and fridge and pulled out a box of organic crackers and a tub of cashew cheese and arranged everything on a blue plate.

The group in the living room erupted in a chorus of cheers. One guy held up a box of typewriter ribbons. You'd think they'd found a wallet with a hundred-dollar bill.

Max nodded toward the group. "Like kids on Christmas morning." From his tone, he didn't approve of their glee.

"I'm going outside for a smoke," I said.

"I'll join you," he said.

"What about the meeting?" I said, looking into the living room, hoping to get Wade's attention to let him know I was going outside, but he was all caught up in new typewriter hoo-hah. "I thought you were into this."

"I just let them use my place."

He sounded detached and strange, but I couldn't say why. Max and I sat on his stoop and smoked.

"One thing I don't miss," I said, "is how every other person you used to see on the street was fixated on their phones. Crossing streets even."

"Pedestrian accidents have plummeted," he said.

A lone airplane grumbled overhead, specks of red blinking between the stars. Two planes in one night. It reminded me of the eighties, when I was a kid and phones had lacy cords you played jump rope with, the days before anyone but Al Gore and his buds surfed the net. Now the challenge for most people was what to do with all the extra time.

Max stamped out a hand-rolled. The yard smelled good from the herbs, fresh. When he worked at Google, the yard was all dirt, no grass, no plant life.

He nodded at our empty bottles. "Get you another?"

"I'm fine," I said.

"I'll get us something else. Be right back," he said.

Max reminded me of the guys I was usually attracted to—handsome, charming, smart. I felt different around him than I did with Wade. Max was intriguing, but if I were with him, I'd constantly worry about keeping him interested. If there was a way to have a secret affair with him, I would. But affairs never stayed secret for long.

The night was so quiet. I preferred noise, cars barreling down the street, the groan of buses. I even missed the clatter of Angel's Muffler Service across the street from my apartment.

A raccoon family skittered along the top of the brick wall between Max's yard and his neighbor's. One raccoon glanced my way, stopped for a moment, causing a traffic jam, then the family continued on their way.

The screen door slapped behind me, making me jump. On the step above where we sat Max set a tray with two shot glasses, a bottle of Jack Daniel's, and a bar of Godiva dark chocolate. A few of my favorite things. I thought of that old song and how happy everyone seemed back then. There were problems. My parents' adultery, for one. But the country was still on its way up, not on its way down.

He poured us shots. In the distance, the faint sound of typebars hitting paper. Happy sounds. I hoped none of the neighbors would hear it. Max pointed to his yard where, with the help of the moonlight, rows of fluffy plant life stood.

"Oregano's over there, rosemary's over there, and the basil is doing really, really well, amazingly well."

"Are you the same Max who used to get all teary-eyed talking about harvesting metadata?"

He rambled about how this was better because he was depending on himself again, connecting with people instead of with their data.

"We went too far," he said. "There never should have been a smartphone."

"I loved my iPhone," I said.

"We all did," he said. "But things had to revert. We needed a hard stop."

"We got it," I said. I needed to get him off this track of iPhones because it only made me miss mine more. "Wade doesn't buy that the Russians did this."

"That's what some people think." He downed his shot and wiped his mouth with the back of his sleeve.

"It's still against the law in this country to kill journalists, but for how much longer? The next best thing is, take away their tools. First the computer, then the typewriters, printing equipment, copiers."

He nodded but had nothing to add.

I broke off a piece of the dark chocolate. "Tastes like strong coffee," I said. "You're spoiling me."

He looked at a chocolate square and laid it on his tongue. "You doing okay with money?"

"I still have some savings," I said.

"Move in here. I have an extra bedroom."

"I don't think Wade would like that."

"Is he supporting you? Paying your bills?"

"Well, no."

"Then why give him a say in where you live? Consider it." Max held up the bottle of Jack. "Dark chocolate is good with whiskey," he said, and poured another shot. I still hadn't finished my first one.

He peered out over his garden as if he were looking for something.

"Remember when you could find a typewriter in mint condition on Craigslist for around two hundred dollars or less?" I said. "We thought *that* was expensive."

"The good old days," he said. "I need a typewriter. Mine conked out. My handwriting is hideous."

"I can try fixing it for you," I said.

"It's beyond fixing," he said. "I dropped it."

"How did you drop it?"

"My brother-in-law's a cop. He stopped by and in my rush to hide it, I tripped over a pair of shoes, and it went flying."

"You really think your brother-in-law would arrest you for owning a typewriter?"

"Let me put it this way: he gave his own wife a speeding ticket."

"That's harsh," I said. "Didn't I meet him once? Looks like a young Sean Penn?" He had a distinct hooked nose, red hair, and eyes so blue they were almost white.

"That's him," he said.

I thought of the typewriters in my second bedroom. I had a protocol: Through friends of friends, people applied for a typewriter. I was good at finding machines—in attics; in the trash, thrown out by people who were afraid of getting caught. But I liked Max—a little too much—and I wanted to give him one.

He stood and stretched. "Want to see my Brussels sprouts?" he said, and gave me a semi-drunken, jokey leer. "C'mon. Bet you never saw them growing out of the ground."

"I've led a sheltered life." I followed him down a row to what looked like miniature palm trees.

"Ta-da," he said.

"They're so cute," I said. "I had no idea."

"Check out this rhubarb."

He pointed at three husky plants with huge stalks and leaves as big as Swiss chard.

"I call them the Three Killers," he said. "Leaves are poisonous. It's the stalks you use for pie. I'll make you one sometime."

"You're not going to poison me, are you?" I said.

"Woman pretty as you? Never."

I glanced back at the house. Someone stood in the window, watching. Wade. I waved but too late. He'd moved.

The garden was beautiful in the moonlight. If you'd just arrived from another planet, you might think this land was paradise. Faint sounds from the neighborhood drifted by. Something knocking about, the rattle of a wagon, squeak of a porch swing. The fragrance of onions and jasmine, a pinch of sage.

"You'd like living here," he said. "This garden." The moon glanced off his eyes; they shined in the night. I thought of wolves, of wild creatures accustomed to darkness, at home in the absence of light.

"I have a typewriter I can give you," I said. "I reached down to touch a Brussels sprouts leaf.

"Seriously?"

"I have more than I need. I'll bring it over tomorrow."

"How many do you have?"

"Enough to give you one," I said.

"Let me come pick it up."

"It's better if I bring it to you. I don't want to draw attention to the Hideout."

Back inside we joined the group. I knew most everyone but not well. Local activists I'd met over the years. Wade glanced at me with sad eyes. The group talked about how they planned to get the news out there. Because there were no old mimeograph machines to be had, and copiers were also government-regulated, to produce bulletins, everyone would have to type and staple and encourage people to share their issues. That meant they needed typewriters, just as Wade had said. I kept my eyes glued to a yellow canary that perched on a dowel in a cage.

"We'll have to work on that," he said. "Everyone, put on your thinking caps. Where can we find typewriters?" Wade glanced at me then, as if waiting for me to offer mine, but my lips were sealed.

Wade pulled into one of the many open spaces in front of the Hideout. I leaned over to give him a kiss, then opened my car door.

"Wait," he said.

I held the door open a crack.

"What about the typewriters?" he said.

I thought about my dozen there in the second bedroom. There were like my children. Just give them all up?

"I can give you a few."

"Just a few? Everyone in the group needs one if we're going to do this paper."

"I hardly know those people. Do you know for sure they each want to retype the bulletin? They're going to sit there and do that? Are you sure?"

"They were all at the meeting," he said, incredulous.

"That doesn't mean they're all serious," I said. "I'll give you three. Okay, four."

He looked disappointed.

"I'll come by tomorrow for them," he said. "Appreciate it."

But he still looked disappointed.

The next morning, I biked over to Max's with a Hermes Baby typewriter that fit snugly in the front basket. Small, easy to transport by bicycle.

"What a nice surprise," he said when he opened his front door and saw me there.

"For you," I said, and held up the case.

He set it down and hugged me. He didn't let go. He buried his face in my hair and breathed in. "Violet," he said.

I liked how it felt, how *he* felt. But I couldn't cheat on Wade.

"We'd be great together, Zoe," he said.

"I like you, too." I pulled away.

"But you like Wade more."

"It's complicated," I said.

"That's your catchphrase for everything," he said.

I went to the Hermes Baby, set it on the table, and unlatched the cover. He rolled a sheet of paper onto the platen of the mint-green typewriter and typed, "the complicated gal with the dark brown hair leads a complicated life."

He looked up at me.

"Funny," I said drolly.

"Really nice of you to give this to me," he said. "Seriously. I feel special."

"Ah, don't let it go to your head. I'm giving some to the writers, too."

"So, you do have a lot."

"Enough," I said. "Look, I better get back."

He walked me to the front door. "Sure I can't convince you to stay? Want to take a puff? I have good weed."

"I really have to go." There was nothing pressing that I had to do, but the less time I was here, the better. I didn't trust myself with him.

I was out front, turning my bicycle around when Wade pulled his UPS truck into the driveway.

His face looked stormy. "What're you doing here?" He peered down from his high seat behind the steering wheel.

"What're *you* doing here?"

"It's been my UPS route for the last three years," he said. "Remember?"

"I brought Max a typewriter," I said.

"You rode your bike over here for that? He's the last person you should be giving a typewriter. He's not even in the group."

"Why're you complaining? I'm giving you four."

"Is something going on with you two?"

"What're you talking about?"

"I saw you last night out in the garden. I came looking for you and you were back there."

"He was showing me Brussels sprouts, for God's sake."

"That's a good one," he said.

He wouldn't look at me, and when he did his glacial blue eyes made me shiver.

"I have a lot of deliveries today," he said, staring straight ahead, his wrist over the steering wheel.

I spent the afternoon in the second bedroom dusting off my typewriters as I tried to decide which to let go of. I loved my Smith Corona Standard with its retro black lines like an old Plymouth and the Smith Corona Clipper with the little red Clipper plane logo and my Hermes 3000 that reminded me of Howard Hughes's

Spruce Goose airplane. I dusted off the Smith Corona Galaxie with the planet logo that made me think of *The Jetsons*, when I heard a knock on the door. I threw a blanket over the typewriters and shut the door behind me. Wade hardly looked at me.

"How was work?" I got two beers from the fridge.

"No, thanks," he said.

"You're still pissed." I set down the beers.

He paced about the apartment. "You only want to give us four," he said. "Aren't you being selfish?"

"They're *my* typewriters, I get to do with them what I want."

"Does Max know you have all these typewriters?"

"I didn't give him an exact number."

"I have a bad feeling about this," he said.

I squinted at him as if his features had fallen out of focus.

"You're welcome to take four. I'll help you carry them down."

"Just point out the ones I can have," he said. "I'll take them down."

I gave him a Smith Corona Sterling, two Royal Quiet De Luxes, and an Olympia—all good typers I would miss but not too much.

He took me into his arms and kissed me. "Sorry for giving you a hard time. I just wish you hadn't given Max that typewriter."

He took the last typewriter and went down the stairway. From the landing, I watched him carry it to his Jeep. That's when I heard the sirens. They sounded too close, that hysterical whirring and shrieking, and then two police cars pulled into the parking lot. My heart rattled and my armpits grew damp.

A cop with red hair got out of one of the squad cars, when it hit me: Max's brother-in-law. He pushed Wade against his Jeep and patted him down. I was about to have a conniption. That was my boyfriend getting pummeled down there.

I was such an idiot. Why hadn't I listened to Wade about Max? Idiot.

I almost ran down there to help, but Wade wouldn't want that. I'd be of no help to him if I got arrested too. I grabbed the backpack that contained a change of clothes, toiletries, and the handgun Wade gave me, along with a sleeping bag that sat by the front door, ready for an occasion like this. I also grabbed my lightest typewriter, the Olivetti 22, and headed down the back steps. My bike stood in the carport where my car used to be. I set the Olivetti in the bike's basket, got on, and pedaled down the alley away from the sirens, which kept coming. The days of the internet now seemed like such a halcyon time.

My mouth went dry, and I was scared out of my wits. I pedaled as fast as I could down side streets and alleys. I had no idea where I was going. I found myself at the end of Wilson Street. I pulled into Canyon Park and coasted down the hill to where a settlement of homeless people lived. The bike slowed to a stop. A little boy trundled up to me, his mother close behind. He smiled, his baby teeth gleaming white, new. The sky turned violet as the sun skidded toward the horizon. Twilight and the first star broke through. Then another.

ONE'S COMPANY, TWO'S A CROWD

The worst heat wave of the summer settled in and shocked me into remembering other hot and humid summers. Only this one was worse and not just because of the pandemic. Earth was heating up. Fires everywhere, the desert hotter than ever, rolling blackouts. It wasn't sleeping weather either, especially when my air conditioner sounded like a leaf blower and threw out tepid air. All the residents here at the Coral Seas apartments also yearned to survive the heat, as evidenced by the pool sign-ups. Because there was no knowing who was contagious, we had to take turns swimming, and people who never gave the pool a second thought were now flapping about for their time in the water.

At two in the morning, I went out onto the landing outside my second-floor apartment. Traffic on Placentia Street beyond the parking lot was light for a Saturday night. On prepandemic nights, after the bars closed and drunk drivers hit the streets, the police cars' carnival lights made me feel like celebrating something. Now, everyone stayed home. Police must be bored. Poor babies.

But not everyone stayed in. Prowlers and burglars were busy. Nothing kept them in.

This morning my neighbor Carmina called across the courtyard: "Sandy, can you talk?"

I put on my mask and went over.

"A man was looking into windows last night," she said, "but I could not see his face. He wore a mask."

Masks kept us safe from the virus, but they also made it almost impossible to identify the bad guys.

"He scared me." She adjusted the elastic around her ears. Her mask had big red embroidered flowers against a turquoise background.

I leaned on the railing in front of her apartment. Below, her kids frolicked in the pool.

"It's so risky," I said, "to go looking into windows, such close quarters and all. Who would do that?"

A former motor court built in the sixties, the Coral Seas's, dozen apartments huddled around a swimming pool that had never been cleaner. The sparkling water must have puzzled the birds used to its murky depths. A small white board hung in the kumquat tree where residents signed up for swim times. Since March 18, when Orange Countians were ordered to shelter in place, the swimming pool had become vital. Residents chipped in whatever money they could to hire a pool cleaner so we could get exercise and the children could expel energy. My boyfriend, Wyatt, a swimmer, chipped in the most money.

It was the middle of the night, and I would've loved to jump in to cool off, but Jesús, the manager, turned off the pool light at midnight. I hoped, because it was Friday, he would leave it on. More than five months since lockdown, and we needed escape hatches at all hours.

Instead, I sat on my little stool and lit a clove cigarette. All the lights of the compound were off, allowing me to stay hidden and watch the goings-on, which was often a lot of nothing. Someone lugging a case of beer up the steps. A couple staggering from their Uber. Barry Manilow crooning for all the swooning ladies who had no idea he was gay, or didn't care.

Right after I thought, *Nothing much happens around here*, a figure wearing a baseball cap and a mask crept around the ground floor corner, went up to the corner apartment, and peered in, hands clasped behind their back as if they were window shopping. I gasped, drew on my cigarette, my hand shadowing the orange coal to prevent from being seen, and put it out. I eased off the stool so it wouldn't creak, but I must have made a noise because the prowler looked up, saw me, and ran off.

Damn.

I was tempted to run after him, but by the time I made it downstairs, he'd be long gone. I lit back up and paced about, pissed off someone was prowling around where I lived.

After I smoked it down to the filter, I went inside and fell asleep on the couch to the old classic film *The Big Heat*, apropos viewing for the weather had made a bad situation worse.

The following morning, I ran into Carmina in the laundry room. Sweat from the ninety-five-degree heat glued the masks to our faces. I should have planned better and done my wash when I learned of the impending heat wave. Wyatt said I've never been good at planning.

"That's how I ended up with you instead of a rich guy," I said, and poked him in the side.

I clicked the washer setting to cold, wishing I could shrink down and jump in with my clothes. "I saw him," I told her.

"Who?" Carmina spritzed herself with a little spray bottle attached to a tiny plastic fan that whirled.

"The guy! Last night he was looking into the window of the corner apartment downstairs."

"New lady lives there. Curly red bob. *Muy bonita*. She has salon but it is closed."

I held a clump of my hair that reached down my back, almost to my waist, and studied the ends. "I could use a trim." A haircut would give me a reason to talk to her.

"Maybe someone on the way home from the Tiki Bar?" She moved her wet clothes to a dryer and inserted two quarters. The bar was still open at night, despite the ruling that closed most dives.

"And what—forgot where he lived?" I said.

Carmina shrugged. "It's not right."

"I don't like it." I poured in soap.

"I will make you gazpacho. It's good on hot days. Cools you down."

That night Wyatt came over for dinner. He was still in his work uniform: gray T-shirt, gray shorts. He delivers furniture, an essential business says our governor. He lives alone and when he's not with me, he doesn't see anyone else. On the job he wears a mask, so we assume—hope—we're safe.

When he came in I said, "Wash your hands," and he singsonged, "I know," making the word "know" skim board the sound waves. He went straight to the bathroom sink, and the faucet ran too long.

"Your hands are clean by now," I called. He loved wasting water.

I was by the front door, looking out, when he emerged.

"What're you looking at?" he said.

"There was a prowler last night."

"Here?"

I pointed in the direction of the downstairs apartment.

Wyatt wrapped his arms around me from behind. "I'll peep on you anytime."

"Not funny," I said.

"It's probably just an old boyfriend who wants back in."

"Just?"

"I don't mean it like that."

His breath was sweet on my neck, a mixture of bubble gum and Mountain Dew.

"That's a creepy way to go about it," I said.

"Not everyone has my manners," he said. "I'd ring the doorbell."

As it grew dark, a faint breeze swept into the apartment. Wyatt opened a couple of cold beers and handed me a bottle. I guzzled. More than one and my inhibitions go right out the window.

"It's so hot," I said, and pulled off my tank top, flung it down the hallway in the direction of the hamper. Wyatt did the same. From all that furniture moving, his six-pack was coming along quite nicely.

Wyatt had to get up early for work. I couldn't sleep. Alcohol and the pandemic were a bad combo. I went out on the landing and lit up a smoke. A few apartments on the second level still had lights on. Not so much on the ground floor.

I put out the butt and was about to go back inside when the prowler reappeared. A short stocky guy. He hung around the same apartment, peeped in the windows, but he didn't try to see if any were open. Didn't try the door. The beer gave me courage. I crept down the stairs. I had to catch the sucker. I didn't know what I would do when I got him, but I moved as stealthily as I could. I hit the bottom step of the laminate stairway and was rounding the pool when I slipped on a Styrofoam pool toy and yelped. The dude heard me and disappeared around the apartment building.

The next morning after Wyatt left, I was out on the landing with my coffee when the ginger-haired woman in the corner apartment went outside, pulling a chair behind her. She brought out a little cart on wheels with haircutting implements, tied a scarf around her head to hold up her curls.

Moments later a young man or woman, I couldn't tell which, sat on the stool. The client wore a mask, as did the stylist, who also wore high heels. She shaved the side of her client's head while the other side remained an inch or two long. Clipped the hair at their neck, took cash, and the customer left.

This went on for the next two hours, during which time I made a fruit salad, smoked two or three cigarettes, and wondered what the heck was going on with the peeper. Maybe one of her clients had become obsessed with her. She *was* pretty, at least from a distance. It was time to take a stroll.

I went downstairs and introduced myself. "I'm Sandy," I said. "I live upstairs in eleven." I pointed.

She said her name was Holly, and she cut hair outside because the salon was off limits. I said I needed a trim, and she said, "What about now?"

Now was fine.

As Holly trimmed my ends in the blazing September heat, I said, "Someone was hanging around last night, looking in your window."

Her scissors went still.

"My window?" She sounded stricken.

"The night before, too. Didn't look like he was trying to get in, but he wanted to see in. We had a peeper around here a couple years ago. Maybe he's back."

"Shit," she said, and jabbed me with the scissors.

"Ouch!" My hand shot up to my wound. I examined my fingers. No blood.

"I'm so sorry," she said. "Maybe it was my ex. It was a bad relationship. I moved here to start over."

"We've all been there." I rubbed my neck.

"What with the restrictions loosening up, I go out some, but I never bring anybody home. Oh, God, if it was my ex . . ." She paced about, her red strappy stilettos scratching against the pavement.

Maybe I shouldn't have told her.

"This world is so crazy," she said. "When will this damn pandemic be over?"

She wasn't asking as much as she was pleading. She handed me a mirror. "I guess this doesn't help you see the back, but it looks good."

I paid her, said I was glad we met, and went back upstairs.

That night I was in my usual spot on the landing, smoking a butt, waiting, but it's like that old saying, a watched pot never boils. The peeper didn't show up. Wyatt delivered furniture to a store in Arizona and probably wouldn't come by. Around midnight, I went in and was at my kitchen table paging through an *Audubon* magazine, imagining being a crow and flying away from here, when I heard the squeak of footsteps on the landing. Maybe Wyatt finished early and made it by. I peeked through the blinds and my eyes met the eyes of Squeaky Shoes. I gasped, he backed off. I jumped up and ran to the door. Lock it or run after the creep? I ran onto the landing, but he was already on the ground floor, powering past the pool.

Wyatt came by the next evening for dinner. Since the pandemic, gone were our dinners out, such as they were—the local taco place or vegan restaurant.

When he came in, he could tell something wasn't right.

"Baby, what's up?" he said.

"The prowler was here."

"Where?"

"Here!"

He shook his head. "That's not good."

"No kidding."

"You call the police?"

"What're they going to do? He'd be long gone by the time they got here."

Wyatt nodded, went to the fridge for two beers, and handed me one, not before tapping it with his own as a toast.

"The new neighbor gave me a trim yesterday."

"Looks good." He squinted at my hair. "Turn around."

"Bullshit. You didn't even notice. That's not the point anyway."

"I noticed." He pulled me to him, picked up a horse tail's worth of my long hair and studied it.

I took my hair back and frowned. "Something is off. I'm worried about the creep wandering about. What if he's dangerous?"

"The last time you worried about someone, you almost got yourself arrested."

"What—would you prefer I ignored people in trouble? Is that what you'd like?"

"Actually, yes," he said. "I would like that very much."

"You got yourself the wrong girl."

"Let's enjoy our night," he said. "Worry later."

In my galley kitchen we made bean tacos and a green salad. We sat on the landing and ate, a respite from the apartment, which felt like a sauna. A breeze stirred. The kids shrieked in the pool below as we enjoyed the violet sky. As the sun died away, Holly's apartment remained dark. There was no way to know if she was in there or if she'd gone out.

Wyatt and I finished off a bottle of chardonnay, when he said, "It's so hot. I feel like taking a swim."

"Kids got the pool," I said.

"Feel like a shower?"

"Let's."

Afterward, he went to bed—he'd been driving all day. I pulled on a sundress and went out on the landing with my smokes. I listened to podcasts, watched YouTube videos on my phone. Time melted.

It was after midnight when the peeper returned. The hair on my arms and neck stood up. I was ready for him. The door opened from the inside of Holly's apartment, and he walked right in. Vague blue shadows played on her walls. Maybe the TV. I remembered she'd said she would not bring anyone inside, so what was up with that?

I grabbed my phone, stood outside my apartment, and put on my mask. There was movement inside Holly's apartment and the sound of something breaking. Someone yelled. I didn't have to think about it, I went on alert. Shapes moved against her walls. Had to be the same stocky guy as before, the one who'd been creeping about. I ran downstairs, and as I did, I saw the dude hitting Holly with the red stiletto heels she wore when she cut hair.

I ran inside, hefted a ceramic sculpture that sat on a shelf by the door, and knocked him upside the head. He called out, a rather feminine tone to his voice, and crumpled onto Holly's carpet. Holly began crying. What a great night for Wyatt to turn in early, damn him.

The dude splayed across her floor as I called 9-1-1. He was out cold. Soon the sirens were upon us, which brought some of the residents outside. They watched from behind masks. The EMTs rushed in. One said, "What happened?" and I told her.

Another pulled off the dude's mask and revealed not a dude but a dudette. I looked at Holly.

"My ex-girlfriend," she said. "Didn't like that I left her, but she had this awful temper." Her voice trailed off.

"Obviously," I said, gobsmacked.

"Girls beat up girls all the time," Holly said. "You'd be surprised."

Not much surprised me anymore, but this did.

The police arrived and took my statement and Holly's just as Wyatt approached. He gave Holly a polite nod.

The policewoman said I could go.

As we trudged up the stairs, he said, "You were right. I should've listened to you."

"What can I say?"

We crawled into bed, and he pulled me to him, and we fell asleep like that, sweaty and close.

51 WINFIELD

The original sign, SUKI THE QUEEN OF BLOW DRIES, still hung in front of Lauren's shop with the addition of a placard that read, COLLECTIBLES. The brick building had been a salon until Suki bleached her husband's lover's hair with Clorox. Suki was arrested, and the salon was forced to close. Which was when Lauren rented it. She had reached the tipping point with her *stuff.* When she couldn't get from the bedroom to bathroom of her small apartment, she knew it was time to declutter or open a shop.

Her mother said, "You're thirty-five years old! You need a husband, not a thrift shop."

"I don't want a husband."

"A boyfriend, then. I have a nice man you should meet."

Lauren said, "No, Mom. I tried that. Not interested." Her mother was full of advice she didn't take. A man wouldn't make her happy unless that man was Scott.

Simply seeing the items her late husband Scott Winfield had loved, and touching them—the typewriters and vinyl records and old stereo equipment—made her happy. Lauren's psychiatrist prescribed Valium, which was supposed to make her happy, but it hadn't helped. There was happy, and then there was *happier*. She was happier when Scott was alive.

One boyfriend, right before she dumped him, said, "You can't let the bastard go."

So what if it were true? All she had left of the past were things from the happiest period of her life. Photographs approximated, but the things he loved were real, and all she had left of him. She didn't even have his remains because he was lost at sea.

She'd given away his old stereo speakers that no longer worked, sold old cameras he'd collected but hadn't loved. Some things were more problematic: his vintage Harley-Davidson, the collection of autographed baseballs, and old license plates from all fifty states. These were treasures, things Scott had loved, which she now loved.

Lauren appreciated old things, the more vintage the better. She joked that's one reason she loved Scott—he was twenty-one years her senior. Interesting things made with care when things were still made with care. Things from her life with Scott and from before she was born, way before. She told her psychiatrist it would help if she knew what happened to him. Five years ago, her fifty-one-year-old husband, Scott Winfield, an experienced offshore sailor, didn't return from a sailing expedition. She visited psychics who were said to bring messages back from the dead, but the psychics couldn't find him. It was as if his soul had sailed to another universe.

The clutter in her house wasn't enough to fill the shop, a redbrick and plate glass building, so she went to storage-locker auctions and estate sales. She trolled flea markets and traversed the alleys of upscale neighborhoods the day before trash day, when rich people put valuable stuff out by the trashcan. Whatever she couldn't use, she donated or left out back in her own alley, where it was swallowed up by people in the night.

She unlocked the front door of her shop to let herself in and locked it behind her. It was early, not even 8:00 a.m. The store opened at 9:00. The smell of incense from the day before—she burned it to cover up the used-items smell—still permeated the air, making her sneeze. It was either that or Clementine, the resident ginger calico that lived here and took care of the rodent population. Clementine slinked in like liquid fur from the back room and rubbed up against her, meowing once to say hello.

"Hungry?" Lauren hefted the slim feline and carried her to the kitchenette in back where she spooned wet food into Clementine's dish. The cat ate like a dog; she took big bites and ate fast, as if afraid the food would be snatched away.

Lauren found a microfiber cloth on top of the vintage white Frigidaire and walked through the shop, randomly dusting. Dust moats floated in the spikes of sunlight that streamed in through the plate glass window. She dusted the mismatched dishes, vintage sequined sweaters, and old tape recorders no one wanted anymore.

She found old things fascinating, which made them hard to sell. Those items she was particularly attached to—pastel aluminum tumblers like the ones her mother poured Kool-Aid into when she was a kid, shoes and coats like those her father wore—she priced high, figuring if someone was willing to pay twice what they were worth, they deserved them. She was aware that this was not how you were supposed to do business, that shoppers might find similar things for less at flea markets or on eBay, but she didn't much care.

Her attachment to things wasn't as risky as forming attachments to people, especially after losing Scott. She had come to think of the flannel zebra jammies, in mint condition, and the grandpa-style gator shoes as friends of sorts. But she also liked the characters who tromped down the aisles, people with limited funds who hoped to find surprises, boutique owners looking for treasures they could resell at higher prices. If only things could talk. If only they could tell her their stories, where they came from, whom they belonged to, and what they did before arriving at her shop.

As Lauren ran her dust cloth over a vintage chrome toaster, she heard whispering. She looked over her shoulder. If someone had come in, why hadn't the bells on the door jingled? And how could anyone get in, anyway? The door was locked.

She heard the voice again, a woman whispering, "Not too dark, Caleb. You know I like my toast golden brown."

She picked up the toaster, looked in and under it.

A man's voice this time, saying, "Darlin', I know what you like." A slight Southern drawl, thick with the heat of summer and Spanish moss hanging from the branches of cypress and oak trees.

Lauren was intrigued, yet at the same time it worried her. Maybe she was having a bad reaction to her medication. She went over to the display case that held estate jewelry. Rhinestones glimmered as if smiling. A pair of lime-green Swarovski crystal earrings winked at her. Could that be right?

She tracked back. She had woken up with a minor headache, symptoms of a blind migraine. She was used to optic migraines; her vision breaking up into prisms of color no longer scared her, but she had never hallucinated voices. She made a mental note to google "migraines" to see if there was an aural version.

At 9:00 a.m., opening time, she reversed the CLOSED sign and unlocked the door. A woman Lauren recognized from previous visits stomped in and dropped a pile of men's shirts on the glass counter and said, "Lousy creep of a boyfriend. When will I learn?"

"His shirts?" Lauren touched the top one. They were of a nice quality, and vintage: mostly bowling shirts with names like STAN and BILL across the pocket, a few vintage Hawaiian.

"Told him if I ever caught him cheating, I'd change the locks. I did, and I did. Helps that I'm a locksmith."

"That's a valuable skill to have," said Lauren.

"I'm selling his good stuff and donating the rest. These are a few of his better garments. Make me an offer."

Three vintage Hawaiian shirts and nine bowling shirts. Lauren didn't spend time going through them but liked the colors and fabric. She smelled them. No musty fragrance.

The woman leaned on the counter, looking blasé. "They're clean. Want 'em?"

"What were you hoping to get?"

"What're they worth?"

"Twelve shirts, all vintage, all in good condition."

"Great condition," the woman interjected.

"How's fifty dollars?"

"Fifty? For all of them? I can get more on eBay."

There was that "e" word again.

"I can give you seventy-five," Lauren said. "Or we can put them on consignment and when they sell, you'll get sixty percent of the sale price."

The woman drummed her fingers on the glass, considering. Lauren went through the rest of the shirts. She gasped when she came to one with 51 WINFIELD embroidered across the shirt pocket. Scott Winfield wasn't a bowler, in fact he hated bowling, but he was fifty-one when he was lost at sea. She believed in signs, and this was one she couldn't overlook.

"How's one twenty-five?" Lauren needed the shirts—specifically that one.

"Really?" the woman said.

"Really!"

"I'll take it!" she said, and Lauren paid her the money.

After the woman left, Lauren set aside the one that said "Winfield," an aqua rayon garment in mint condition, to explore later and examined the shirts more carefully. Each one gave her a distinctly different smell or taste. The bright orange Hawaiian shirt with neon-green palm trees elicited a taste of mint. The darker-hued sunset shirt smelled like musk. The one with tropical fruit splayed across the fabric suggested pineapple. The rest smelled like the woods or snow or spring. One, with images of swimming pools and high dives, stung her nose with the smell of chlorine.

She tagged them and put them on hangers. Now she was ready for Winfield. She gently handled the aqua shirt, circa mid-fifties. Black stitching ran around the bottom hem and sleeves. She brought it up to her face and breathed in the salty ocean air.

Then she heard, "Baby." A man's voice that sounded so much like Scott's tenor.

Her heart rate picked up. Things were becoming decidedly strange. Hearing, smelling, and tasting inanimate objects? She should talk to someone. Her psychiatrist was out of town. She hadn't read the material that accompanied her meds. Perhaps she had better. She went to the water cooler, poured a glass, and drank.

The store filled with shoppers. The city's local alternative weekly had recently given her store a nice review and business had picked up.

Fifty-one Winfield lay on the display case. A customer whizzed by, backed up, and pointed.

"Ooh, look at this, Rondo," a teen with purple hair said to his flamboyant friend, whose head was shaved on the sides with rooster-like tufts standing straight up from his skull.

Lauren pretended to be busy arranging the jewelry in the case, but her attention was ratcheted. Had they heard what she heard? The one named Rondo looked at the tag.

"Large," he said. "Nah." He let it drop onto the counter.

They wandered off to the rack with the other shirts recently placed there. She took 51 Winfield and pressed her face into it once more.

"I've missed you," the voice said.

Scott always said he'd come back to her. It had been five long disturbing years.

"Took you long enough," Lauren said into the shirt.

At 6:00, she closed the store and took the shirt into the back room. She fed Clementine, poured a glass of wine for herself and another for Scott. She propped the shirt on the chair across from her and set the glass of wine on the table before it.

Clementine inhaled her food. Lauren sipped and studied the shirt.

"Thanks for the wine," he said, "but I can't drink anymore. I don't know how."

"Oh," she said. "Are you okay? What happened to you? What happened on that boat?"

"Ah, it's a long story, m'dear."

"I've got nothing but time."

"Okay, then," he said, and told her the story of how the water was rough the day he sailed from the Newport Beach harbor. A few miles out, gale force winds came out of nowhere. When he went on deck to reef the sails, the boom swung across the deck, hit him in the head, and sent him overboard, just like that.

"I shouldn't have gone by myself," he said.

"You were always stubborn about that," she said.

"I loved the feel of being on the ocean alone, all that open space around me," he said.

"But you're okay?" she asked.

"Now I sail all the time."

She finished her wine, and his, then took the shirt and lay down with it on the office futon. They talked deep into the night. She caught him up on everything important that happened since he left. And when she finished, just before she fell asleep, he said, "I'll see you right here tomorrow night," and she said, "It's a date."

That night she dreamed of the ocean, the deep purple phosphorescent waves after the sun went down; the metallic cast the water took on, making it look frozen in time; and a sailboat, thirty feet long, with a teak deck.

When Lauren awoke, she kissed the shirt, made herself presentable, and fed the cat. She hung the shirt beside the fridge. The store crowded with customers, and she was friendlier than usual because she had Scott back. It didn't matter that she couldn't see him. She could *feel* him. She had his company. Some might think she was crazy, so she didn't tell anyone. Her mother visited her father's grave every week to talk to him. Lauren was lucky; she could talk with Scott every night, and she didn't have to talk to a silent grave. She had her husband back. She would never need anyone else.

POOL FISHING

The sun lumbered over the auto body shop across the street and a scrim of pink outlined its corrugated roof. The pool below my apartment turned my favorite color, sea glass, masking the murk all too apparent at high noon.

In my galley kitchen, I tipped Mr. Coffee over my cup and went out onto the landing. From my apartment on the second floor of the Placent_a Arms—the manager threatened to get the "I" fixed—doors opened and gardeners and construction workers emerged. The still-fresh air smelled of salt from the ocean a mile away. When the Costa Mesa *fabricas*, auto body shops, and *taquerias* got busy, exhaust and fried-food smells, not altogether unpleasant, replaced the salty fragrance.

The swimming pool drew my attention. On the surface of the water a Bud beer bottle bobbed about, not so unusual at the Arms, but the bottle looked stopped up with a plastic bag. Odd.

I retied the belt of my bathrobe and hurried down the prefab stone steps. The bottle was too far out to reach, so I used the leaf sifter pole to draw it in. I hoped no one was watching. Silly, a grown woman circling forty, fishing bottles from a swimming pool. I returned the sifter to its place and tucked the trophy inside my robe, cold against my bare skin. The gravel-embedded laminate felt slick on the bottoms of my feet as I rushed back upstairs.

My boyfriend, Wyatt, knew about my pool fishing obsession. He said I was the most unusual woman he knew. I had goldfish as pets and subscribed to *Fish World*, *Wrestling*, and *Popular Mechanics*. I stored my credit cards taped inside old magazines slumped in the rack, and my idea of a good time was volunteering at the soup kitchen up on 19th Street, not shopping. Please, no shopping. Online ordering worked just fine.

I used a pair of long tweezers to pull out the plastic bag, then set the bottle in the yellow shaft of light. A little slip of paper lay on the bottom. I dumped it out, along with a cigarette butt. I unfolded the little slip of paper with no expectations of what I would find. Prince Charming chain-smoking his worries away, wondering where I was?

I didn't just rescue beer bottles. Beside my fifty-five-gallon fish tank, leaning in the corner were a tricycle, an antique metal toaster, and a baseball bat.

A police helicopter groaned overhead, common in Westside Costa Mesa, known as Costa Misery to those of us biding our time here. I decided the smeary letters were an "E" and a "P" and another "E." Moisture blurred the ink. I held the paper up to the light.

The words "Help me" came into focus. *Help me?*

It had to be a joke, designed by someone who knew I fished things out of the pool. Wyatt. He did it, just to get my goat. He got me good.

I left the bottle in the middle of the table, along with the slip of paper, and spent the day futzing around. Wyatt came over at six to fetch me for dinner—our weekly date at Wahoo's Fish Tacos. Big spender, my Wyatt. I observed his expression as his eyes landed on the bottle.

"Either you're drinking earlier and earlier," he said, "or you've gone pool fishing again."

"Very funny," I said, and waited.

He waited, too. "What?"

"What do you mean, 'what'? You didn't do that?" I gestured at the bottle. "Stop playing with me already."

"I love playing with you." He pulled me close, running his fingers under my T-shirt and further north.

I told him about finding the bottle, but he was rubbing me up here and down there, the way I like it.

"You missed your calling," I said, although I didn't exactly know what I meant by that. I kicked the door shut and we stumbled across the hardwood floor to the sofa where Wyatt continued to do what he did best.

As we showered, soaping each other's backs and fronts and underneaths, I said, "Somebody's in trouble."

"One of your neighbors is playing with you." He soaped my arms. "A neighbor sees you fishing things out of the pool, gets bored, and thinks, who can I mess with? You, that's who."

"I don't think so." I rinsed off and stepped onto the red bathmat. I wrapped myself in a red bath sheet. "I can feel it. Something's wrong."

He turned off the water. I handed him the other bath sheet.

He followed me into the living room. Late-day sun slotted in through the blinds. The pool shone below, all turquoisey and bright, as if we were at a lux Orange County resort and not a converted motel on the misery side of town.

"I can't just do nothing," I said.

"You're so dramatic." He came up behind me.

The sky was the color of plums. Streetlights on Placentia, beyond the parking lot, flashed on. Three crows perched on the phone wires above the street.

"Look," I pointed. "Those same crows were there this morning in the same place."

"You sure?"

"I'm sure."

"Damn." He let out a breath. Wyatt didn't believe in much, but he did believe in crow symbolism. Those muscular black birds didn't scare me—I thought they were beautiful—but they scared Wyatt, who was at least six foot tall and had arms like river rocks from moving pianos. But his fright happened on the inside, which his brawny self couldn't protect.

At Wahoo's I scanned the menu. You'd think I'd have it memorized by now. I ordered fish tacos with guac on the side. Afterward, we went to Goat Hill Tavern and got drunk on martinis. Wyatt's good that way: Whichever way I'm headed, he's by my side.

We were both too drunk to drive, so we called an Uber, and as the Prius pulled up to my not-so-fancy home sweet home, I squinted at the Arms's sign.

"You think anyone notices the burned-out 'I'?" I said to Wyatt.

"What 'I'?" he said.

In the parking lot, the newest resident, a burly dude with long sideburns, in jeans and a denim vest, jumped from a 4X4 truck you needed a ladder to climb into. He hunched over as he carried a six-pack of Bud and a bouquet of supermarket flowers up the steps.

"Wyatt," I said, stumbling from the cab.

He paid the Uber driver and followed me to the stairs.

"Hmm?"

"That guy." I gestured in Burly Dude's direction. He disappeared through an apartment door.

Wyatt's attention swerved to the opposite direction. On the corner adjacent to the Arms, cop car lights whirled about, a dizzying holiday. A shiny low rider with yellow stripes flanking the metallic purple side idled by the curb. A cop had the Latinx driver up against the car, frisking him. The west side of Costa Misery had a huge population of Latinx people, which the police hassled more than whites.

"This place is so racist," I said, moving in their direction, but Wyatt held me back.

"Down, girl."

I needed to stop reacting without thinking. It would get me into trouble someday.

Upstairs, the August heat of the apartment closed in, so we left our clothes in a puddle on the floor and jumped in the shower where we did more than bathe.

Wyatt left at sunup, but not before he said, "Top of the morning to ya!" He moved pianos for a living all over Southern California. I was thinking about Burly Dude with the beer and flowers. I still had a bad feeling.

At the table I sat with my coffee. My apartment afforded me a view of apartments on both sides of the U. Just when I thought nothing would happen, Burly Dude emerged from his door on the far end. He stomped down the steps, making my apartment vibrate, started his 4X4, and drove away.

I pulled on a pair of jeans and T-shirt, slipped into flip-flops, and moseyed onto the landing. Already the heat was creeping upward. I padded to Burly Dude's apartment and listened. Next door, Marta emerged, shouldering a tote bag with spray bottles.

"Hey, Marta," I said. "Do you know the guy who moved in there?"

She frowned. "You mean *couple*? He not so nice to his lady."

"What do you mean?"

"She cry. A *lot*. Sorry. I have to get the bus. Rich people need clean houses." She tapped her tote brimming with cleaning fluids.

At Burly Dude's door, I pressed my ear against it. Bleeding through was the distinct sound of a morning TV show and what sounded like a human cough. I tried the doorknob, then knocked. Nothing. Knocked again. There was the muffled sound of moaning, someone trying to call for help but having trouble getting the words out. I jiggled the knob. There was a little give.

I ran home for something to pick the lock. When my older brother was a kid, he taught me how to pick locks—preparation for his later life of crime, which moved him to his current happy home, Chino State Prison.

Back at the door, I stuck my crochet hook into the lock, and miracle of miracles, the door opened. I gave a little push. An apartment layout just like mine—big rectangular living room, tiny kitchen. A vase holding the flowers Burly Dude carried home last night. The bedroom door was closed. I went to it and listened. *Good Morning America.* It squeaked open. On a straight-backed chair, a young woman in a football jersey with the number 42 was tied up, duct tape over her mouth. Her dark eyes were as big and round as malted milk balls.

I went to her and peeled back the duct tape.

"He's coming right back," she said. "Went out for food."

"Why'd he tie you up?"

"Tried to break up with him. You should go."

A pink comforter covered the bed. A clock radio sat on the nightstand, framed photos on the dresser.

"Does he always keep you tied up in here?"

"Just when he goes out."

"I'll be back," I pressed the duct tape back onto her face.

As I eased out of the room, the truck pulled in. I locked and closed the door to the apartment. I was at the top of the stairway by my place when Burly Dude reached the top. Any second my heart was going to explode out of my chest.

He smiled but his eyes held no light. A heart tatt decorated his muscly forearm, and he carried a Del Taco bag. "Morning," he said.

"Morning."

I rushed into my apartment and watched through the venetian blinds as he unlocked the door. He noticed something was different, but not different enough to stop him. Crows sat on the phone lines. I had to do something, but what?

I called the police and told my story to the dispatcher, who said she'd send someone over when an officer freed up.

"What part of woman tied up in a chair don't you get? How long am I supposed to wait?"

"We'll have someone there just as soon as we can." She sounded tired and jaded.

"I swear," I groaned, and tried calling Wyatt but got his voicemail.

My heart wouldn't slow down. I broke a sweat—from the heat of the day or my upset, maybe both.

I scanned the apartment for something I could use for protection, if necessary. A dumbbell was the only thing I owned that could do serious damage. Gurgling from the tank drew my attention. The air filter had come loose again. I tightened it as Wanda and the other fish skimmed the top of the tank, looking for food. As I replaced the lid, I saw it, the baseball bat. Better than a dumbbell. Easier to swing.

I sat and paced, sat and paced, all the while keeping a watch on Burly Dude's apartment. Doors opened and Hispanic women and children poured out—going to their cleaning jobs, walking kids to school. Finally, Burly Dude's door opened. He got back into his truck and growled away. I took the crochet hook and baseball bat that leaned in the corner and hurried to the apartment, all the while praying to St. George, the saint of courage and bravery, that I would rescue the woman before I shorted out from a case of nerves.

I picked the lock and was in the apartment before anyone else left their apartment. When I opened the bedroom door, the woman's wide eyes said, *Get me the hell out of here.* I peeled back the duct tape.

"Thank God," she said.

"Where'd your boyfriend go?"

"Ex-boyfriend," she said. "He's a process server, had papers to serve."

I undid the knots.

"He's a nice guy, except when he's mad. He was always throwing beer bottles into the pool. You were always fishing them out, and I had to try."

I undid the last knot. "How long have you been in this chair?"

She got up, kicked out her limbs, and ran into the bathroom. "Days!" she called. Then she was in the kitchen, downing a tall glass of water. Her arms wore purple splotches.

"He do that to you?"

"He was upset I was leaving."

I felt my face grow red. "We should go," I said, throwing the baseball bat over my shoulder. "You have someone you can stay with?"

She was taking her time in the kitchen. Maybe she didn't want to leave. Women could be like that, not want to be set free. I stood watch at the front door. She ran to the bedroom and bathroom and was still throwing things in a bag when the truck roared into the lot.

"He's back," I said.

She joined me, an unzipped backpack hanging from one hand. She chewed the fingernails of her other hand.

He was out of the truck and on his way.

"C'mon." I pulled her along, having no idea what we were going to do when we saw him.

We were out on the landing when he hit the bottom step. He was busy watching his feet when he looked up.

"What the fuck?" he said.

He picked up his pace. He was on the landing before us.

"Natalie," he said.

When he grabbed at her arm, I held the bat as if I were about to swing at a ball.

"Hey," I said.

"I swear, Nat, I'm gonna kick your ass over this," he said.

Natalie began crying.

"Take the back stairs." I jabbed the air with my index finger. "Now."

Burly Dude and I faced off. He grabbed at the bat, but I've always been fast on my feet, and when I'm mad, there's no stopping me. I jumped back in time. He grasped at air.

"Guys like you ruin it for the good ones." I let the statement hang in the air between us. I backed up into the far corner, out of the office's line of sight. He came at me. I swung at his knees, and he fell. He pulled himself up, and I thought of Natalie's bruises and of my best friend's sister in Alabama whose husband had strangled her, wrapped her up in plastic, and buried her in the woods behind their house.

Who else would Burly Dude hurt if I didn't do something?

"Bitch," he said, and that's when I saw stars. Name-calling triggered something in me because my vision shattered into gray and white shimmering splotches. I swung the bat against his skull, hard. He looked surprised. I pushed at his torso as hard as I could with the tip of the bat, and when that wasn't enough, I dropped the bat and used my hands. He grabbed onto the railing but lost his footing and flipped over. His skull bounced against the bullnose edge of the pool.

Down below, Natalie screamed and scampered out of the office, followed by the manager. They bent over him. I joined them, and soon the EMTs and police were everywhere.

They agreed it had been an awful accident, and after I spent the day at the police station, they released me. Wyatt was waiting, still in his work clothes, hands deep in his pockets.

"What the hell?"

"I had to help a neighbor."

"You must've done more than that for them to bring you here."

"The guy with the Bud and the flowers. He fell from the landing, and I was a witness, so they brought me in."

"*Accidentally* fell?"

"He threatened his girlfriend, then he threatened me. He lost his footing and fell. That's it."

We hurried from the Costa Misery police station to the car across the street. Wyatt's mouth fastened into a frown.

"He was a rat," I said.

Wyatt beeped the remote to unlock his Tundra. He opened the passenger's door, and I climbed in.

"He was holding his girlfriend hostage," I said. "I had to do something."

He breathed out hard and gave me a sidelong glance. I would never tell Wyatt or anyone what had really happened. I couldn't. The world was better off with one less rat. I would soothe myself with that thought, which at first would be often, and then, not so much.

ACKNOWLEDGMENTS

I would like to thank David Olsen and Kelp Books for giving my stories the perfect home. I couldn't be happier with the book's gorgeous cover created by Travis Barrett and Christian Claudio. Thanks to my critique group, the Authors of Ambiguous Intentions. I'm grateful for my writing instructors and advisors at Goddard College—G. Roy Levin, John Dranow, and Kathryn Davis—who believed in me long before I believed in myself. So many more friends and students, too numerous to mention, who've cheered me on. You know who you are, and I thank you from the bottom of my heart. Much love to my son, Travis Barrett, for always believing in me, and my partner in life, Brian Barrett, for your bottomless optimism and endless support. You mean more to me than you'll ever know.

Photo credit: Travis Barrett

Barbara DeMarco-Barrett is the *Los Angeles Times*–bestselling author of *Pen on Fire: A Busy Woman's Guide to Igniting the Writer Within*. She is also author of *Palm Springs Noir* (Akashic). Her work has appeared in *Coolest American Stories, Orange County Noir, USA Noir: Best of the Akashic Noir Series, Dark City Crime and Mystery Magazine,* and *Rock and a Hard Place*. Her Pushcart Prize–nominated story, "Rowboat," is included in this collection. She is creator, executive producer, and host of the award-winning podcast, *Writers on Writing*. Visit penonfire.com to learn more.